"BECAUSE ON CHRISTMAS EVE, THEY'RE GOING TO PUT THE ANIMALS TO SLEEP."

The Fabulous Five stared speechlessly at the man as if he had just pronounced their own doom.

Finally, Melanie broke the silence. "No!" she cried, pushing out her chin.

"No, what?" the man asked, looking at her with surprise.

"No, we're not going to let anybody put these dogs and cats to sleep," she answered defiantly.

"Do you have the money to adopt them, or homes for them?" he asked.

Melanie's shoulders sagged, and she looked at the faces of her friends. They all looked horrified, and Mona's cheeks were wet from the tears that were running down them.

"We'll find a way," Melanie said with conviction. "Come on, gang, let's go have a meeting at my house." She'd find a way to save the animals before Christmas Eve if it was the last thing she ever did.

THE FABULOUS FIVE

The Christmas Countdown

Betsy Haynes

A BANTAM SKYLARK BOOK®
NEW YORK · TORONTO · LONDON · SYDNEY · AUCKLAND

RL 5, 009–012

THE CHRISTMAS COUNTDOWN
A Bantam Skylark Book / November 1989

*Skylark Books is a registered trademark of Bantam Books, a
division of Bantam Doubleday Dell Publishing Group, Inc.
Registered in U.S. Patent and Trademark Office and elsewhere.*

ISBN 0-553-15756-6

Published simultaneously in the United States and Canada

---

*Bantam Books are published by Bantam Books, a division of Bantam Double-
day Dell Publishing Group, Inc. Its trademark, consisting of the words
"Bantam Books" and the portrayal of a rooster, is Registered in U.S. Patent
and Trademark Office and in other countries. Marca Registrada. Bantam
Books, 666 Fifth Avenue, New York, New York 10103.*

PRINTED IN THE UNITED STATES OF AMERICA

CW   0 9 8 7 6 5 4 3 2 1

For Rosemary Johnasen,
the world's greatest animal lover

CHAPTER

1

"Come on, guys. Help me think," Melanie Edwards pleaded with her friends Katie Shannon, Jana Morgan, Christie Winchell, and Beth Barry. The Fabulous Five were seated in a corner booth at Bumpers, the favorite after-school hangout for kids from Wakeman Junior High. "I want a puppy for Christmas so badly. I'll die if I don't get one."

"Why won't your parents let you have one?" asked Beth, fingering an earring shaped like a miniature Christmas tree.

"They say it will have to be housebroken, it will howl all night, and it will need a lot of taking care of. I told them I'd get up with it when it made noise, take it for walks, and do *everything* for it." She twisted a strand of her reddish-brown hair between her fingers as she talked.

"What did they say to that?" asked Christie.

"My mom just gave me her all-knowing smile, and my dad stuck his head back into his newspaper."

"Why don't you get a cat, Mel?" asked Katie. "Our cat isn't that much trouble. Libber just sleeps all the time."

"I don't *want* a cat. I want a *puppy*," insisted Melanie, scrunching her eyebrows together in a determined frown.

"I remember when we first got Agatha," said Beth, referring to her family's old English sheepdog. "Boy, was she ever a pain. She howled all night and ran around the house breaking things. She even knocked down the Christmas tree. *Twice*. Come to think of it, she really hasn't changed that much. She knocked it down again yesterday. But in my family, she just sort of blends in."

"You're no help," Melanie said, sighing.

"Shane Arrington's sitting over there. Maybe if you asked him, he'd get Igor a wife and you could have one of the baby iguanas," suggested Jana.

"*Gross!*" squealed Melanie. "You're no help at all. You don't understand how badly I want a warm, furry puppy. I'd give anything for one. I'd even give up going to school for a year, if I could have one."

"Wow! What a sacrifice," said Christie with a grin. "The next thing you know she'll be willing to give up baby-sitting her little brother."

"I'll bet there's one thing she isn't willing to give up, even for a puppy," said Katie.

"What's that?" asked Jana.

Melanie slid deeper into the booth. She knew what was coming next.

"*Boys!*" Katie said. "There's no way she'd ever give up flirting with boys."

Melanie made a face at Katie, but deep down she wasn't really angry. Her friends teased her all the time about how much she liked boys. But when she really needed The Fabulous Five, they always came through for her. The five of them had been best friends ever since they all went to Mark Twain Elementary School together.

"Hey, Melanie, there's Mona Vaughn with Matt Zeboski," called out Beth. "She goes to the animal shelter all the time to play with the cats and dogs. I'm sure she'd have a good idea about how you can get a puppy."

Melanie watched as Mona and Matt joined the line of kids waiting to order food. Mona had been visiting the animal shelter three times a week for over a year. She had once told The Fabulous Five that her family couldn't afford to have a pet of their own so she made up for it by going to the shelter to lavish her affection on the unwanted animals who lived there. Sometimes she even brought liquid bubble-maker and blew bubbles into the cages to entertain them.

"Right," said Jana. "Maybe you could get one for free."

"And you could make your mom and dad feel bad for not wanting to help a *poor, little, homeless* animal right at Christmastime," said Christie. "You know, peace on earth, goodwill to dogs."

Melanie's spirits leaped at the suggestion. "Sure, and if I pour it on heavily enough, it might work."

"I'll give you some acting tips, if it will help," volunteered Beth. "You can even borrow my makeup to help you look *really* sad."

"She doesn't want to overdo it the way you did when you tried to get your parents' attention by making yourself up to look as if you were injured," said Katie to Beth. "All that got you was grounded."

"Let's call Mona over," said Christie, waving to get her attention. Mona saw the signal and headed for their booth.

"Hi," she said when she reached them.

"Melanie has a problem," said Katie, "and we wondered if you could help us."

"Sure," said Mona, her face brightening. "You know I'll help you guys do anything if I can."

"I want a puppy for Christmas and my parents don't want to get one for me. You go to the animal shelter all the time, and we wondered if they have any cute puppies and what it costs to get one," said Melanie.

"Oh, they've got *lots* of cute puppies and kittens, but I don't know what they cost. I'm going there right after I leave here, though, and I'll ask."

"Can I go with you?" pleaded Melanie. "I'd love to see them."

"Me, too," said Jana. "Why don't we all go? Would they let us in?"

"Sure. There are always people there looking for pets. I'm leaving in about twenty minutes. I'll stop at your table on my way out."

A little while later, Mona led the way as they all filed into the foyer of the animal shelter. A Christmas tree stood in one corner. Melanie smiled as she looked at the decorations on it. There were squeak toys, rubber balls, dog biscuits, and an assortment of other colorful playthings hanging among the branches. She could hear yelping and barking in another part of the building. Suddenly she felt sad. Christmas was less than two weeks away, but it didn't make any difference to the animals. Most of them would probably still be stuck in their cages at the shelter.

"Oh, hello, Mona," said the heavyset lady at the desk. "Is it Wednesday already?"

"Yes, Mrs. Graham. I was wondering if it would be all right if my friends went back with me to see the animals?"

"It sure would. Maybe they would each like to take one home with them."

"Don't I wish," said Melanie, sighing deeply.

The six of them trooped through the door behind the desk, and the barking immediately became louder. Melanie opened her eyes wide at the sight. Chrome-wire cages, with green plastic garland hanging along the tops, were stacked double along the concrete-block walls. The bottom cages had larger dogs in them and the upper ones had smaller dogs. In the center of the room was a double row of stacked cages. Most of them contained cats of assorted colors and sizes. A young man wearing a baseball hat sideways was scrubbing the tiled floor with a bucket of water and a broom.

Melanie had never seen so many cats and dogs at one time, and many of the dogs were pawing at the bars of their cages as if they wanted the girls to come to them. There were large dogs with loud, deep voices and small dogs with chirpy little voices that bounced around like squeak toys. There were long-haired dogs and short-haired dogs.

There were lots of kittens, too. Some were gray, some were black, others were calico, and there were even a couple of expensive-looking Siamese cats. They all turned and looked silently at the girls as they walked by. One kitten stuck its paw through the bars and swatted at Melanie's finger when she pointed at it.

"Oh, I love every one of them," cooed Melanie.

"Me, too," Mona agreed. "That's why I come to play with them every Monday, Wednesday, and Friday after school."

"The puppies are *so* adorable," said Jana. "How could anyone bring them here?"

"They are cute," said Mona. "But I like the older dogs and cats, too. They get neglected sometimes, and I can hardly stand the looks on their faces." Her own face brightened. "Let me introduce you to my favorite."

Mona walked to the end of the row of cages on the right. In the very last one on the bottom was a multi-colored dog that lay with its chin resting on its paws. Its fur had blotches of brown and white and black, and there was even some red. When the dog saw Mona, it sat up and its tail swept back and forth across the floor of its cage like a whisk broom.

"Hi, Rainbow. How are you today?" Mona asked the dog sweetly, sticking her hand in the cage to be licked.

"I call her Rainbow because of all her colors," she said. "She's been here for a long time, and we've become *very* good friends. If my mother would let me, I'd take her home."

Melanie looked at the dog's large brown eyes. They

seemed so calm and accepting. She reached into Rainbow's cage and stroked her head. Her hair was soft and fine.

"I wonder how much they charge to take one home," Melanie mused.

"Adopting an animal costs twenty-five dollars."

Melanie and the others turned to the young man in the baseball cap who had spoken. He was leaning on his broom watching them. "That goes to pay for all of the shots and things we give them here."

"Are many people taking them home for Christmas presents?" asked Melanie.

"Yeah, about four or five animals are adopted each day," he answered. "But if you want that one, you'd better get her real soon."

"Why?" Mona asked, her voice quivering.

"Because on Christmas Eve day they're going to put a bunch of the older animals to sleep. As you can see, we're completely filled up, and nobody comes in after Christmas wanting a cat or dog, but the animal-control warden keeps picking up strays and bringing them in. We'll need the space for the new ones. I expect she'll be one of the ones that gets put to sleep."

The Fabulous Five and Mona stared speechlessly at the man as if he had just pronounced their own doom.

Finally, Melanie broke the silence. "No!" she cried, pushing out her chin.

"No, what?" the man asked, looking at her with surprise.

"No, we're not going to let anybody put them to sleep," she answered defiantly.

"Do you have the money to adopt them, or homes for them?" he asked.

Melanie's back stiffened. She looked at the faces of her friends, and they all looked as horrified as she felt.

"We'll find a way," she said with conviction. "Come on, gang, let's go to my house and have a meeting." She'd find a way to save the animals before Christmas Eve if it was the last thing she ever did.

CHAPTER

2

"Okay, what are we going to do?" asked Melanie after The Fabulous Five and Mona had gathered in the Edwardses' family room. Her six-year-old brother, Jeffy, under strict orders to mind his own business, had planted himself directly in front of the television. He was watching a cartoon Christmas special with the sound turned low.

"You're the one who said we were going to do it," said Beth. "There must be forty or fifty dogs and cats at the shelter. How in the world are we going to save all of them? It would cost at least a zillion dollars."

"We don't have to save *all* of them," responded Katie. "Just the ones they're going to put to sleep."

"I can't stand the thought of their putting Rainbow to sleep," said Melanie, looking at Mona. "She's so sweet."

"I wonder if they would give us a group rate?" mused Christie. "You know, half price if we take so many."

"That's a *great* idea!" exclaimed Melanie. "Let's ask."

"The first thing we've got to find out," injected Jana in a practical tone, "is how many animals we're talking about. That man said they were just going to put some of the older ones to sleep. Does that mean ten? Fifteen? Twenty?"

"They probably won't know for sure until they find out how many animals are adopted before Christmas," said Mona. "I could ask Mrs. Graham. She might be able to give us an idea about approximately how many there will be."

"Why don't you call her now and find out?" suggested Melanie. "You can use the phone in the kitchen."

"While Mona's calling," said Katie, "why don't we talk about what we'll do with them if we're able to get them."

"Give them to kids at Wacko as Christmas presents?" suggested Beth. "I'd give one to Keith if he didn't already have a dog."

"Maybe he'd like a cat," said Christie.

"I think that's a good idea, but Randy has a dog, too," said Jana. "And Heidi's been around so long that she'd probably be jealous of a new animal."

Katie looked at Beth. "Couldn't you use your stage makeup kit and dress them up like kids and enroll them at Wacko?"

Beth laughed. "Now *that's* not a bad idea."

"We could tell everyone that they're Laura McCall's friends," said Christie, throwing her head back and laughing. "They've just gone to the dogs."

"No," protested Jana. "I don't think we should let the poor animals keep such bad company. It wouldn't be good for them." Everyone went into fits of laughter, and Melanie hung on to Christie, she was laughing so hard.

Laura McCall was the leader of a rival clique that called themselves The Fantastic Foursome. Laura and her friends had given The Fabulous Five trouble from the first day they had started seventh grade at Wakeman Junior High.

"What about asking kids at school if they want one?" asked Melanie, wiping the tears from her eyes. "Maybe some of them have already asked for pets for Christmas. All we have to do is convince them to have their parents get them from us instead of the pet store. I'll bet once they understand, lots of them will do it."

"We can ask," agreed Jana. "I'll check with Mom and see if she'll let me have a kitten."

"Mrs. Graham says there will probably be about fifteen," said Mona, coming back into the room with a sad face.

"Fifteen," said Christie quickly. "Fifteen times twenty-five dollars is, let's see . . . that's three hundred and seventy-five dollars."

"Oooh," moaned Beth, slapping her hand to her forehead. "That's a lot of money."

The group went totally silent. For a moment they just looked at each other.

"Do you suppose we could get a bank loan?" asked Melanie softly.

"No way," said Katie. "What could we use for collateral? The bank always wants to know what they can have if someone can't pay them back."

"We could all put up our bicycles," suggested Beth.

"I don't think any bank would go for that," said Christie. "Besides, mine's not even worth ten dollars. It belonged to both my older brothers before I got it."

"Did you ask Mrs. Graham if they give discounts if you take a lot of animals?" Jana asked Mona.

"She said she didn't know. No one has ever asked

that question before. It costs the shelter more than the twenty-five-dollar adoption fee to give the animals shots and take care of them. The rest of the shelter's money comes from donations. She'd have to ask her board of directors if they could give a discount."

They looked at each other. Melanie had run out of ideas.

"We could baby-sit and pool our money," said Beth, sitting up quickly.

"That would take forever," said Christie. "We've only got until Christmas Eve. Besides, I still have more presents to buy."

"And there are only ten more shopping days until Christmas. That means we've got nine days between now and Christmas Eve day," said Jana. "What we need is a way to earn a lot of money really fast."

"Let me think," said Katie, chewing on her lower lip. "I don't know the exact figure, but three hundred and seventy-five dollars is between sixty and seventy dollars *each* for the six of us. None of us has had that much money at one time in our lives."

Gloom settled back over them.

"*I've got it!*" yelled Melanie, jumping up. "You're absolutely right," she said, pointing at Katie. "That is a lot of money for just the six of us. But it would be less for each person if there were more of us." The others stared at her.

"Don't you see? If we ask some of the guys such as Scott Daly, Randy Kirwan, Keith Masterson, Shane Arrington, Tony Calcaterra, Jon Smith, and Matt Zeboski to help out, we could get the money a lot faster."

"I noticed you only mentioned boys," said Katie. "We do have some girlfriends who might help, too."

Melanie put on her most innocent expression. "We can ask girls if you want to, Katie. I just thought we'd start with the people that would be most fun. Don't tell me you'd *mind* having an excuse to be around Tony."

Katie's face turned beet red, and she didn't reply. Melanie knew Katie was totally embarrassed at the mention of Tony. Katie pretended she didn't have a crush on him, but everyone knew she did.

"That's a great idea," agreed Christie. "And I'll bet if someone asked the principal, he'd let us put up a table in the cafeteria to collect money for the animals."

"Would you do it, Christie?" asked Melanie. "You've got an in with him." Melanie cringed the moment the words were out of her mouth. Christie hated to be reminded that Mr. Bell and her mother were good friends because they both were school principals.

Christie shrugged. "Oh . . . okay. It's for a good cause."

"It's still a lot of money to raise," said Jana, "and most kids are broke from buying Christmas presents. But if we try, just *maybe* we've got a chance to get it."

"I hate to be a party pooper," said Katie. They all turned to look at her. "Suppose we *are* able to get the money. We still haven't answered the big question. *What are we going to do with fifteen dogs and cats?*"

CHAPTER

3

"You want us to do *what*?" asked Tony Calcaterra, looking at Melanie with a surprised expression on his face.

It was the following afternoon and Tony, Keith, Randy, Scott, and Jon were squeezed into a big corner booth with The Fabulous Five and Mona at Bumpers. Shane was leaning against the side of the booth, and Matt was standing next to him.

"We want you to help us earn money to free some dogs and cats from the animal shelter. They're going to be put to sleep on Christmas Eve if no one buys them," said Melanie.

"That's right," insisted Beth. "Those poor animals

will die while the rest of the world is singing carols and opening presents." She cast her eyes down for dramatic effect. Then her face brightened a little and she said, "You should see them. They're *sooo* sweet and adorable."

"I've got a better idea," said Shane. "Why don't we bake some dog biscuits with metal files in them and sneak them into the animal shelter?"

"Yeah," said Keith. "The animals could saw their way out, and we'd have a getaway van waiting outside."

"With fake tags to give them so no one would know they were escaped convicts," added Randy.

"And Igor could be the getaway driver," Shane offered. "He'd love it. He watches cop shows on TV all the time, and the chase scenes are his favorites."

"*Guys!*" said Jana. "We're serious. We've *got* to help these poor animals."

"That's right," agreed Christie. "Do you want their deaths on *your* consciences?" She looked sternly at each of the boys.

"Look," said Melanie. "It won't be hard to earn three hundred and seventy-five dollars if we work together."

"Three hundred and seventy-five dollars?" asked Matt, his voice rising in disbelief. "That's a lot of money."

"And we can't wash cars or mow lawns," said Randy. "It's winter, remember?"

"Right," agreed Keith. "Besides, what would we do with fifteen cats and dogs, anyway? Don't think you're going to ask me to take two home. My mom and dad would kill me, even though it is Christmas."

"My mom and dad work and wouldn't want one either," said Jon.

Melanie looked down into her lap. What to do with the animals once they had saved them had been worrying her, too. In fact, it was just as big a problem as raising the money. They couldn't buy fifteen dogs and cats and just turn them out onto the street.

"Let's not worry about that now," Melanie said, crossing her fingers behind her back. "We'll give them away at school, or something. We'll figure that out later, but first we've *got* to find a way to earn money to save them."

"We don't have much time," said Tony. "Christmas is only ten days away."

"It was ten days from *yesterday*," corrected Katie. "It's *nine* days from today."

"I said I'd talk to Mr. Bell to see if we can set up a table in the cafeteria to ask for donations," said Christie. "Lots of charities make appeals during the Christmas season because people are in a giving mood. I'm sure that if I explain that to Mr. Bell, he'll let us."

"That's a good idea," Shane agreed. "Would he let us make an announcement over the public address system, too?"

"Maybe," answered Christie. "I'll ask."

"What about advertising in the newspaper?" asked Katie excitedly. "You know, we could prepare one of those ads that really tugs at the old heart strings. My mom could write it, if your mother can get it in the newspaper, Jana."

"That's a great idea!" responded Jana. "Since my mom's the classified ad manager, she could probably get it in. And we can include information about where people can send donations. Whose address shall we put in?"

No one said anything for a moment, and Melanie held her breath. Her parents might not like it if they found out she was involved in a scheme to rescue dogs and cats, especially since she had been begging so hard for a puppy of her own for Christmas. Still, no one else was volunteering, and it would be a couple of days before donations would start coming in and they would have to find out. Surely she could think of something to tell them by then. Taking a deep breath, she said, "People can send the money to my house."

"Good. I'll ask Mom to work on our ad tonight,"

said Katie. "Since she's a free-lance writer, it won't take her any time at all."

"If you call me, I can copy it over the phone, and my mom can take it to work with her in the morning," said Jana.

"I'll make up a schedule for sitting at the donation table," said Melanie. "Two of us at a time can take care of it. We'll have a boy and a girl there each day," she added, looking at Shane out of the corner of her eye.

"I'll make a poster to tell people what it's all about," said Beth.

"I'll make a sign-up sheet for kids who want a cat or dog," joined in Christie.

"And I'll ask Mrs. Graham if she would please talk to her board of directors to see if they will give us a discount," said Mona, her eyes sparkling with enthusiasm.

"Great," said Melanie. "And then we can all meet by the fence in the morning and make our last-minute plans."

"One for all and all for the dogs," said Keith, raising his cola cup high in the air.

"And for the cats, too," said Mona as she bumped his cup with hers. They all cheered.

On the way home, Melanie thought about the pet project and wondered if she was getting herself into more than she could handle. It was one thing to want to help save the animals, and there was no question that she was determined to do that. But her parents would have a fit when they found out that the donations were being sent to *their house*. And what about finding places for all the animals once they had been adopted? Was she being too optimistic in thinking that people would volunteer to take them? she wondered.

On the other hand, she thought, smiling to herself, there were some good things about rallying so many kids to work together, also. For one thing, it gave her the chance to be around Shane and maybe even to impress him with what a kind and caring person she was. After all, he loved Igor, and he seemed very interested in saving the dogs and cats. Surely he would like her more than ever for being involved in such a worthwhile cause.

"Oh, Melanie!" Mrs. Miller, the widow who lived next door to the Edwardses, called just as Melanie was turning up her sidewalk.

"Hi, Mrs. Miller." Melanie noticed the older lady had a worried look on her face.

"Hello, dear. Have you seen my Duchess?" Duchess was Mrs. Miller's Pomeranian dog. It was small with a pointy nose and long blond hair, and Mrs. Miller kept a little pink bow between its ears. She treated Duchess, who was old, too, as if she were her baby.

"No, I haven't," Melanie replied thoughtfully. "Has she been missing long?"

"I let her out in the backyard a couple of hours ago, and when I went to let her in, she wasn't there. I don't know *how* she could have gotten out. The gate was closed and locked and there are no holes under the fence."

"I'm sure she'll come back when she wants her supper, Mrs. Miller. But I'll keep an eye out for her, just in case."

Melanie's mother was in the kitchen, as usual. Mrs. Edwards liked staying home with her children and hadn't had a job outside the home since before Melanie was born. She baked cakes and pies a lot, and the house always smelled yummy when Melanie came in from school. Today, she and Jeffy were decorating freshly baked Christmas cookies.

"Hi," Melanie said, putting her books on the kitchen counter and snitching a warm cookie off the platter where they were cooling.

"Hi," her mother responded cheerfully. Then her expression clouded and she added with a sigh, "Honey, please don't walk off and leave your books there. You know how much trouble I have keeping this counter cleared off."

"And Santa's watching," said Jeffy, shaking a finger at her.

"I won't." Melanie sat on a stool at the counter

and munched on the cookie. "Mrs. Miller just told me that Duchess ran way."

"Oh? When did that happen?" her mother asked.

"She doesn't know. She put her out back, and when she went to let her in, she was gone. Mrs. Miller says there aren't any holes under the fence."

"I bet she'll show up at her front door wanting to come in any minute now."

"That's what I told her. I hope so, anyway. It would be terrible if she lost Duchess right at Christmastime."

Melanie was quiet for a moment, choosing her words carefully. "Uh, Mom."

"Yes."

"After school yesterday, The Fabulous Five all went to the animal shelter."

"Oh? I think I know what's coming, and no, you can't have a puppy. They're a lot of trouble to take care of, and I would be the one who would have to do it."

"But the animals at the shelter are going to die if someone doesn't take them. A man who works there told us that they have to put some of them to sleep because they don't have enough room, and they're going to do it on *Christmas Eve*."

Her mother turned to look at her and wiped her hands on her apron. "Look, sweetheart. There are a lot of animals in this world that need taking care of, I don't deny that. But there's no way we can take care of all of them."

"Not even one?" Melanie asked softly.

Her mother shook her head.

"What if it were a grown-up dog? It wouldn't be much trouble, not like a puppy."

"Melanie, please. I've got enough work to do. Any kind of a dog needs to be let in and out, fed, watered, and walked. I just don't have enough time for it."

Melanie sighed. This certainly wasn't the time to tell her mother about the plan to save the animals.

Later in her room, Melanie looked out her window, watching the snow fall softly. Under the streetlight in front of her house she could see Mrs. Miller. The older woman was walking toward one end of the block, calling out her dog's name. At the corner she turned around and walked in the other direction and called again. Melanie pressed her face to the window. She could see Mrs. Miller's footprints in the new snow, but no tiny paw prints were anywhere to be seen.

Oh, no, thought Melanie, Duchess must still be missing. She vowed to call Mrs. Miller in the morning. If Duchess still hadn't shown up, Melanie would look for her on the way to school. Maybe she'd also suggest that Mrs. Miller put an ad in the lost-and-found section of the newspaper.

With a sigh Melanie sat down on her bed and opened her notebook to a clean sheet. Before she started her homework she wanted to work out the schedule for kids to sit at the cafeteria table and collect money. I'm glad it was my idea to make up the schedule, she thought gleefully, so now I can pair myself up with Shane.

Melanie smiled to herself as a new and even better idea occurred to her. Why not call Shane right now and ask him to help her work up the schedule? She jumped up from her desk and headed for the phone. Working on the pet project could even turn out to be fun.

CHAPTER

4

"There are Randy and Keith," said Melanie, waving to the two boys as they parked their bicycles at the bike rack. She and the rest of The Fabulous Five were waiting at the school fence along with Mona, Shane, Tony, Jon, Scott, and Matt.

"What took you guys so long?" asked Beth.

"Randy had an extra bowl of dog biscuits for breakfast, and I had to wait for him," Keith said with a laugh. "And then he kept chasing cars on the way to school."

"What a funny guy," responded Katie.

"The meeting of the official committee to save the animals will come to order," said Melanie, taking

27

charge. "No more wisecracks until we've finished our business. Christie, did you get to talk to Mr. Bell last night?"

"Yep, and he said we can put up a table in the cafeteria. He thought it was a very good idea, but he wants us to place the table where it won't interfere with traffic. He also suggested we have a money box, and if we want, we can take it to the office, and they'll keep it in the safe for us." Taking a deep breath, she added, "He also ask me if we had homes for the animals, and I told him we were working on that."

Melanie tried not to let Mr. Bell's concern about homes for the animals dampen her spirits, especially since the rest of The Fabulous Five were jumping up and down with joy over being able to put up a donation table in the cafeteria.

"Will they make an announcement over the public address system for us?" asked Jon.

"Yes," answered Christie. "He asked when we wanted to start it, and I said this morning."

Jana announced that her mother had taken the ad Willie Shannon wrote to work that morning, and her mom had said she was sure they would run it as a public service so it wouldn't cost them anything. Beth held up the poster she had made the night before.

"Would the animal shelter let us take pictures?" asked Tony. "If they will and we can find someone who has a camera, we can put pictures of the cats and dogs on the poster and on the table."

"I'm sure they would," said Mona.

"That's a great idea," said Jana. "Let's ask Garrett Boldt. He takes pictures at all the games and is taking the pictures for the yearbook."

"We can take the film to one of those one-hour photo places and get them back the same day," Tony added.

"Did you talk to Mrs. Graham about her asking the shelter board to see if we can get a reduced rate?" Jana asked Mona.

"I called her, and she said she'd ask," answered Mona. "I'm supposed to call her back in a couple of days. She also said that if we do adopt the animals, someone would have to sign an adoption paper for each one, guaranteeing that he or she will take care of it or return it to the shelter. She was really firm about that. She said she thinks it's great that we want to save the animals, but she told me at least three times that we have to find homes for them before the shelter will release them."

Nobody said anything for a moment, and Melanie knew they were all probably as worried about homes as she was. "Shane and I made up a schedule last night," she said, trying to lighten the mood. "I've got copies for everyone. Shane and I will take today."

"I hate to say it, because it might jinx us," said Christie, "but I'm impressed with our plan. We ought to get enough money real quick."

"We'll have enough money in plenty of time," agreed Melanie cheerfully. The way everyone was helping made her feel great. What could go wrong when The Fabulous Five were pulling together and the other kids were helping? They were unbeatable.

"I hate to keep bringing it up again," said Randy, "but Mrs. Graham was right. What *are* we going to do with fifteen dogs and cats?"

Melanie didn't have any better answer than she had before, but she refused to let one detail quench her enthusiasm. "We'll think of something. I know we will. For one thing, we'll put a sign-up list on the table for anyone who wants a pet. We'll have plenty of kids asking for one in no time."

"I wouldn't hold my breath," Randy insisted. "Have you talked to your mom and dad about your getting Rainbow?"

"Well . . . kind of," answered Melanie.

"What did they say?" Randy asked.

"I just need to talk to them a little more. They'll change their minds." Melanie tried to sound confident. "It's only my mom I have to convince."

"Only your mom." Randy laughed. "That's like saying *only* the Supreme Court."

* * *

"What if we put the table next to the door so that the kids can give their leftover change as they're leaving the cafeteria?" asked Shane.

"Good idea," said Melanie, handing the rolled-up poster to Mona and picking up one end of the table. She and Shane positioned it so it could easily be seen by anyone leaving the room.

Mona pressed the poster flat and then taped it to the front of the table while Melanie and Shane dragged two chairs over.

"There," said Mona, standing back and viewing her handiwork. "That ought to get everyone's attention."

"We could put speed bumps in front to slow people down," suggested Shane.

Melanie gave Shane a big grin. "Maybe you could lie down and be one?"

"Are you kidding? With the stampede of kids going outside after lunch, that's a sure way to get killed," he answered, smiling back at her.

"I guess we're ready for business," said Mona, opening the shoe box she had brought to collect the money in. "I want to be the first one to donate." She opened her purse and dropped some change in the box.

"I've got something, too," said Shane, taking a plastic sandwich bag out of his pocket. It was full of pennies, nickels, and dimes. "Don't tell anyone—it might get back to Igor—but I stole this out of his piggy bank. He'll never miss it. The one thing he's not good at is counting."

"Wait a minute," said Melanie, digging in her purse. She came up with a quarter, two dimes, and a nickel and dropped them into the box. "*Now* we're ready for business!"

People started wandering into the cafeteria. Several stopped and read the sign. Marcie Bee and Sara Sawyer were the first to come over to the table.

"Is this what Mr. Bell was talking about over the public address system this morning?" asked Marcie.

After Melanie and the others explained it to them, she and Sara put money into the box.

As the cafeteria filled, more and more kids noticed them and added to the growing pile of pennies, nickels, and dimes. A few dropped in quarters. Some said they'd like to donate but couldn't, explaining that buying Christmas presents had taken all of their money.

Beth, Katie, Jana, and Christie all came with their hands full of change to add to the collection. They each had robbed their banks.

Garrett Boldt came by with his camera hanging from his shoulder, as usual. After he had donated, Melanie asked him if he would take pictures of some of the animals at the shelter. He agreed to meet her and Mona there in the morning.

Melanie was exuberant as she watched the level of money rise in the box. Even though it was Christmas season and most kids didn't have a lot to spare, almost everyone tried to help. She and Shane were having a great time talking to people and explaining what they were doing.

At one point, Laura McCall came by with the rest of The Fantastic Foursome, Melissa McConnell, Funny Hawthorne, and Tammy Lucero.

"What are you doing?" asked Laura suspiciously. She ignored Melanie and spoke directly to Shane.

After he told them, each of The Fantastic Foursome put money into the box. Laura looked back at them as they left.

Even Laura can sympathize with poor, unwanted animals at Christmastime, thought Melanie. Maybe she isn't totally selfish after all.

Melanie stuck her finger in the box of money and stirred it so she could see the silver coins among the copper pennies more easily. At this rate it shouldn't take long to get the three hundred seventy-five dollars they needed. She had a vision of herself opening the door to the cage and Rainbow jumping out to freedom.

CHAPTER

5

"Give me some more pennies!" Beth demanded, and Melanie looked up to see her shaking Keith's arm.

"Get your own. I'm busy counting nickels," Keith joked in response.

Melanie looked around the big oak, pedestal table in the Edwardses' kitchen with satisfaction. Stacks of coins covered its surface. There were silver piles of nickels and dimes glittering under the overhead light and piles of pennies that looked like shingled anthills. Melanie and the others were busy counting and stacking them into neat little pillars while they munched on Mrs. Edwards's Christmas cookies.

Melanie was silently relieved her mother was at the grocery store so they could count the donations without her asking questions about what they were doing.

"I've never seen so many pennies in my life," said Shane. "You'd think *someone* would have thrown in a dollar bill."

"I know," said Jana. "It looks like a lot of money, but it might not be."

"There! I've got the dimes all stacked," said Randy, popping a gingerbread man into his mouth. "I counted six dollars and forty cents."

"Let me write that down," said Christie, scribbling the number on a pad of paper. "How much did we get in quarters?"

"We've only got fifteen quarters," answered Tony. "That's a measly three dollars and seventy-five cents."

"Is that all?" complained Melanie. "I'll bet we put in half of them ourselves." She knew she was right. She had continued to contribute a few cents at a time until half of her allowance was gone, and she noticed Jana and Beth were doing the same thing.

"Yo! I'm finished with the pennies," said Tony, sitting back and smiling appreciatively at the rows of copper coins neatly arranged in stacks of tens on the table in front of him. "Twenty-five dollars and thirty-one cents. And have you ever seen a better-looking bunch of pennies?" he said, cocking his head and admiring his work. "They'd pass inspection at the Chase Manhattan Bank."

"They wouldn't let *you* in the front door of the Chase Manhattan Bank," Keith said sarcastically.

"Not if they wanted to keep the pennies they already have." Shane laughed.

"How much do we have in nickels?" Christie asked, looking at Melanie.

"I've got four dollars and eighty-five cents," she answered.

"That comes to a grand total of, let's see . . . forty dollars and thirty-one cents," Christie announced.

"Wow! That's a lot of money for one day," Melanie said, looking at the table full of coins. If they collected this much every day, they would definitely have enough to pay for the animals.

"Hmm. Let me do some figuring," said Christie. The room was quiet as she busied her pencil. "We need exactly three hundred thirty-four dollars and sixty-nine cents more, and, if we collect forty dollars a day every day, it will take us eight more days to get enough."

"Gee," said Katie. "We've only *got* eight more days, and that includes two weekends."

"Yeah. And one of those days is Christmas Eve day," added Jana somberly.

"Do we still need that much?" asked Mona.

Melanie saw the hopeless look on Mona's face even though Matt reached over and gave her hand a squeeze, and she felt a knot in her own throat. Everyone was silent as gloom settled over the group like a dark rain cloud.

"Hey, wait!" shouted Melanie. "Don't forget we're going to have the ad about the animals in the paper, and Garrett's going to take the pictures in the morning to put on the poster on our table. We're bound to collect lots more money."

"That's right," joined in Beth. "I'll bet we get bunches of money from the newspaper ad."

"And the paper ought to be on the porch by now," said Melanie, running to get it. She still hadn't figured out a way to explain to her parents about the pet project, and time was running out. She would have to come up with something before they saw the ad asking for money to be sent to their own address.

"There it is," she said, spreading the paper on the counter and pointing to an advertisement on page three. The others crowded around to see.

"The money should come rolling in tomorrow or Monday, anyway," said Melanie. "Why, we'll probably be able to donate enough to build a new wing on the animal shelter," she added, trying to sound more hopeful than she felt. "Maybe they'll even name it after us."

"It's still a lot of money," said Randy, rearranging

the stacks in front of him, and Melanie knew he was right.

"Well, *I* think we're going to do a lot better when the money starts coming in from the newspaper ad and we get the pictures of the animals on our posters," Melanie insisted.

Then a new thought occurred to her. "Guys," she said breathlessly. "Listen to this. What if . . ." She paused and looked around the table nervously. What she was going to suggest was a pretty wild idea. She could only hope that the others would go along with it. "What if, instead of giving Christmas presents to our friends, we donated the money we would spend to save the animals."

No one said anything for a moment. Melanie held her breath and crossed her fingers in her lap, but even though she wanted everyone to say yes, part of her was already regretting that she might not exchange presents with The Fabulous Five.

"I think it's a great idea," said Katie. "It would have a lot more meaning than buying the same old sweater or stuffed animal for each other."

"I agree," said Jana. "It's what the Christmas spirit is all about."

"Igor would certainly go for it," said Shane. "He hates the crowds in the malls during the Christmas season."

Everyone was nodding and agreeing, and Melanie felt warm all over that she had such special friends.

"But right now we've got to get this money put away," said Christie. "I'll keep track of what we collect if someone else will take it to the school office for safekeeping."

"I'll take it," said Tony. "I'd like to see the look on Mr. Bell's face when he sees I'm doing something he can't send me to Teen Court for."

"Oh, he knows you've reformed," joked Katie. And then as if she had second thoughts, she said, "But maybe I'd better go with you just to be safe." They all laughed.

"My dad's coming by for me. Do you have a ride home, Your Honor?" Tony asked Katie.

"No, I don't, and yes, I would like one."

"Before everybody leaves, there's still one more thing to talk about," said Melanie, shifting nervously in her chair. "What are we going to do with all of the animals once we get them? *Nobody* has signed up to take one."

"And Mrs. Graham won't let us move them out of the shelter until an adoption paper has been signed for each animal," added Mona.

"Whose parents would be willing to take them temporarily?" asked Christie. "Just until we find permanent homes?"

No one said anything, and most looked at the floor.

"Does anyone have a basement?" asked Mona.

"We have one," said Katie. "But we also have a cat. Libber would go berserk if we put a dozen dogs down there."

Melanie bit her bottom lip. Her house had a basement. Still, there was no way to hide that many animals from her family. Even if the cats were quiet, the dogs would bark.

"We'll just have to keep thinking," she said with a sigh.

The rest of the group got up along with Tony and Katie and started putting on their jackets and sweaters. Melanie put one paper bag inside another for reinforcement and then dropped the coins in. As they were gathering in the foyer to leave, the doorbell rang.

"Hi, Mrs. Miller," Melanie greeted her neighbor when she opened the door. "Why . . . what's wrong?" The older woman's eyes were filled with tears.

"I've looked all over for Duchess and still haven't found her," said Mrs. Miller.

Melanie took the woman's hand and pulled her into the foyer.

"Who is it, dear?" Mrs. Edwards called from the living room. She had just come in the back door with the groceries and was hanging up her coat in the front closet.

"It's Mrs. Miller. She hasn't found Duchess yet."

Her mother came into the foyer. "I'm so sorry, Clare. I was convinced that someone would have found her and returned her to you by now."

"Me, too," said Melanie as the others gathered around. Why hadn't she remembered to look for the little dog on her way to school this morning? She could have walked over to Hickory Street and then gone up Allendale instead of her usual route, and maybe Duchess would have been there waiting for someone to help her find her way home.

"Melanie, why don't you and Jeffy look some more?" asked her mother. "Maybe you can go in a new direction. Come on into the living room, Clare. You can have a cup of coffee with me while they're looking."

"We can help, too," said Jana. "I don't have to get home right away."

"Neither do I," said Randy.

"Me neither," said Shane.

"Hey, that's great!" cried Melanie. "Tony, you and Katie have to go, but everyone else can stay and join our search party. "Don't worry, Mrs. Miller. We'll find her."

"Right on!" said Keith. "We'll form a puppy-posse." He opened the door and raised his arm as if he had a sword and was leading a charge. The others piled out of the house behind him.

They broke up into groups of twos and started tramping through the snow, searching the neighborhood in different directions. Melanie went with Shane, but as much as she was glad to be with him, the little lost dog was all she could think about. They cut through a side street and then went into an alley behind homes calling Duchess's name. They looked in backyards and stood on their toes to see through dirty garage windows trying to find her. Shane threw a snowball at one doghouse, but he retreated quickly when a big Labrador retriever came out and snarled at them.

Finally, after winding their way through streets and alleys for an hour, they returned to Melanie's house, their faces red from the cold air. The others were gathered on the front steps.

"Any luck?" Melanie asked as she and Shane flopped on the steps next to them.

"Naw," said Keith. "I've yelled 'Duchess' so much, I'm afraid I'll start calling Beth Duchess."

"You do and I'll call you Fido," Beth protested.

"I really hate to tell Mrs. Miller we couldn't find her dog," said Jana. "Is there anyplace else we can look? Is there a place she usually ran to when she got loose before?"

"Not that I know of," Melanie said dejectedly. "As

far as I know, she's never gotten out of her yard before."

"We looked all around the fence and couldn't find where she might have dug her way out," said Randy.

"You know what could have happened?" offered Shane. "There are people who steal dogs and sell them to medical research laboratories. Someone could have come along, reached over, and picked her out of the yard."

Beth made a face. "Don't talk that way."

"Well, it's true," Shane insisted. "It *happens*."

"Maybe Duchess was picked up by the dog warden," said Mona. "We could call the animal shelter to see if they have a Pomeranian."

"Good idea," said Melanie. "I'll sneak into my kitchen through the backdoor so Mom and Mrs. Miller won't know we're home. I'd rather wait until we find out if the shelter has her dog before telling her we couldn't find her."

When Melanie reached Mrs. Graham, she said there were no Pomeranians at the shelter. Back outside she reported the grim news.

"Well, I guess we'd better tell Mrs. Miller we couldn't find her dog," said Jon. They all looked at each other, dreading passing on the news.

Just then the front door of Melanie's house opened and Mrs. Edwards and Mrs. Miller came out.

"Did you find Duchess?" asked Melanie's mother.

There was a look of hopeful expectation on Mrs. Miller's face.

Melanie searched for the least painful way to answer. In the brief moment she hesitated, the look of hope faded from Mrs. Miller's face, and Melanie knew she didn't have to tell her a thing. Mrs. Miller already knew the answer.

CHAPTER

6

"**M**elanie!" Her mother's voice calling her sounded stern. Melanie had cleaned up the cookie crumbs and soda glasses from where her friends had been counting money in the kitchen. What else could she be disturbed about? Her mother was standing next to her father's chair in the family room.

"What's the meaning of this?" her father asked, shoving the newspaper toward her. It was opened to the page containing their ad asking for donations. Her heart sunk to her feet. This was it. The moment she had been dreading.

"Uh . . . it looks like an ad about some animals," she said, hoping to bluff her way out of a mess.

"It says that a group of kids are trying to buy cats and dogs from the animal shelter and are asking for donations," said her mother. "It also says to send donations to Miss Melanie Edwards, and it has our address. What in the world are you going to do with a bunch of cats and dogs?"

"Play with them" said Jeffy, who had walked into the room. "When are we going to get them? How many will there be?"

Mr. Edwards frowned at him. "We're *not* getting any cats and dogs."

"We're going to find homes for them," Melanie said, trying to sound positive. "We've got a sign-up list at school and everything. The shelter is getting overcrowded and will put them to sleep if someone doesn't take them."

"Melanie, why didn't you talk to us about this before you started the whole thing?" asked her mother.

"I was afraid you'd get mad and say I couldn't get involved," she answered with her head down. "We were only trying to help some animals who are going to die on Christmas Eve if someone doesn't do something." She felt a big lump starting to build up in her throat, and she knew that she was going to cry. She hated crying, especially in front of her mother and father.

Her parents were quiet for a moment. "How do you know they're going to be put to sleep on Christmas Eve?" her mother asked in a low voice.

"A man at the animal shelter told us, and Mrs. Graham, who works at the desk, says it's true."

"*Humph!*" Mr. Edwards cleared his throat. "Well, uh, if kids are signing up at school to take them, I guess it would be all right. How many dogs are we talking about?"

"Dogs and cats," corrected Melanie. "Mrs. Graham says it will be about fifteen."

Mr. Edwards whistled.

"And you're going to find homes for all of them?" asked Mrs. Edwards.

"*We'll take one each!*" shouted Jeffy.

"No, we won't, young man," his mother scolded. "I've got enough work to do around here without animals under my feet."

"But we'll take care of them," pleaded Jeffy. "Won't we, Melanie?"

Melanie looked at him. Jeffy had fallen to his knees and was clutching the legs of his mother's slacks with both hands. His face was twisted in a grimace as if he were about to cry. He's pretty good, thought Melanie. I should have told him about this before.

"Jeffy, get up," commanded Mrs. Edwards. But she looked as if her resolve was shaken.

"Well, I guess it's all right if you go ahead," she said, "as long as you find homes for them, and I mean someplace else." She turned and went back to the kitchen.

"How many kids have signed up for a pet?" asked her father.

"I don't know. I haven't seen the list lately," Melanie said, dodging the question.

"*Hmmm*." He looked at her a moment and then dug out his wallet. "Here. Just make sure that you find somewhere *else* to keep them."

Melanie looked at the ten-dollar bill he handed her. "Oh, Dad, that's great!" She threw her arms around his neck and kissed him.

Melanie got to the animal shelter ahead of Garrett and Mona on Saturday morning, and while she waited for her friends to arrive, she stood on the top step, watching huge snowflakes drop from the sky and thinking about the predicament she and her friends had gotten themselves into.

Since her parents had seen the newspaper ad last night, she was seriously beginning to worry about what would happen if they collected enough money by Christmas Eve day and then couldn't find homes for all the dogs and cats. Would the shelter refuse the money and put the animals to sleep anyway? It was obvious that her parents wouldn't take them in. Her thoughts rushed to Rainbow. She couldn't let them put Rainbow to sleep. She absolutely *couldn't*! And no matter how much help the other kids were, it was her responsibility. She was the one who had started the whole thing by wanting a puppy for Christmas and coming to the shelter with Mona.

Just then Garrett jogged up the steps with Mona. He waved his camera and called out, "Okay, show me my canine and feline models."

Garrett was an eighth-grader, and Melanie thought he was really cute. In fact, he ranked number three on her crush list, right after Scott and Shane and just before Derek Travelstead. But she didn't have time to think about romance now. She had to save the animals.

"They're inside, Flash," Melanie said. "Let's go."

Mrs. Graham greeted them cheerfully and told them that Charles would get the animals they selected out of the cages for them.

The sound of barking rose to a frenzied pitch as Melanie opened the door to the room where the cages stood. The dogs jumped at their cage doors, as they had when Melanie and the others had come to see them on Wednesday. The cats stared at them and a few meowed silently in the din of barking.

"When you're finished, I'll show you the adoption papers that will have to be filled out if you take any of the animals," said Mrs. Graham. She left them to their picture-taking.

"I don't know which ones to choose," said Melanie. "They're all so cute."

"Why don't we start with that little white dog?" suggested Mona. "I know it's one of the older ones. It's been here a long time."

Charles, who turned out to be the man with the sideways cap, took it from its cage. It was small with cute little button eyes that peeked through its shaggy white hair.

"Oh, it's adorable," Melanie said, holding it next to her cheek. "Its tongue looks like a little pink cookie."

"Do you want to be in the picture with it?" asked Garrett. He had mounted his flash attachment on top of his camera and was ready to shoot.

"No! Not the way I look this morning," said Melanie, reaching up to smooth her hair.

They took the white dog's picture and then the picture of a black poodle that pranced around excitedly on sticklike legs and was hard to stop long enough to snap its picture.

Next Charles took a sleek gray cat and a long-haired yellow one out of their cages, and Mona held them together as Garrett shot a close-up of them in her arms.

They took a picture of a mixed-breed dog that Melanie thought must be a cross between a golden retriever and a dachshund. Blond hair covered its long body, but its legs were so short it looked to her as if it were on its knees.

Garrett took pictures of two more dogs and a cat before asking, "Do you want any more?"

Melanie looked around at the rows of cages and wished they could take all of the cats and dogs out and hold them for a little while. She understood now why Mona came three times a week to play with them. It seemed like such a little thing to do when the animals loved it so much.

"One more picture," she said, looking toward the cage at the far end of the row on the right.

Charles let Rainbow out, and she came directly to Melanie and Mona. Both girls hugged her.

"If I can talk my parents into getting her, you can come and play with her as much as you want," Melanie said to Mona.

Mona smiled and held up her crossed fingers.

"Take our picture with Rainbow," said Melanie.

"I thought you didn't want your picture taken," responded Garrett.

"This is special," answered Melanie, pulling a piece of mistletoe out of her backpack and holding it over the dog's head. Then she and Mona smiled for the camera and so did Rainbow.

On the way out they stopped at Mrs. Graham's desk as she had asked.

"This is the adoption agreement we ask everyone who takes one of our animals to sign. It gives information about the animal, but more importantly it says that the person will feed and take care of their new friend, they will take it to a veterinarian if it's hurt or sick, and they won't allow it to be used for any experimental purposes."

Mrs. Graham continued, "It also says you will tell us if the animal becomes lost, and you will bring it back if you don't want it anymore and not just give it to someone else. The adoption agreement has to be signed by an adult."

"Gee," said Mona, "I didn't know you were so strict. That's great."

"It's almost like adopting a kid," said Garrett.

"We care about our animals," said Mrs. Graham. "If you really do take several of them, we're going to have to have an *adult* sign one of these for each dog and cat."

Melanie stared at the formal-looking paper. It made their project seem even more serious. She had thought they would just pay the money and the shelter would give them the cats and dogs. Well, when they found people to take them, she was sure they wouldn't mind signing a little adoption agreement. But what if they couldn't find enough people? What would they do then?

"I'll take the film over to the one-hour photo lab

and have the prints back this afternoon," said Garrett as they stood in front of the animal shelter a few minutes later. "I'll drop them off at your house," he said to Melanie.

"Thanks, Garrett. You really are super," she said, and then said good-bye to Mona.

On the walk home, Melanie thought again about the adoption agreement. There was no way Mrs. Graham was going to let them pay for all the animals and just take them if there was no one to sign the papers. She thought back to the conversation at her kitchen table yesterday when she and her friends were counting money.

Christie had suggested that someone with a basement might keep the animals temporarily. That wasn't a bad idea, thought Melanie, but no one had agreed to do it. She thought about her own basement again. There was no way that it would work. Her parents had already said that they wouldn't agree to housing fifteen cats and dogs.

Could I *hide* them down there? she wondered, but the instant she thought of it, she knew it wouldn't work. The washer and dryer were in the basement, and she or her mother did a load of laundry practically every day. And besides that, Jeffy rode his tricycle down there when the weather was bad outside. The only other possibility was the room behind the garage that her father used for a workshop.

He hardly ever went out there this time of year, but it was too small for so many animals, and besides, it wasn't heated.

Melanie trudged along in the snow, feeling more dejected than ever. Nothing was working out right. She had been so optimistic at first. She had believed that she and her friends would earn the money quickly and find lots of homes for the animals and she would get Rainbow for her own. She had even thought that she could work on the project with Shane and that he might even ask her out. But none of it had come true. Not the money, not the homes, not Rainbow, and not even Shane.

Shane. Melanie stopped in her tracks. Why hadn't she thought of it before? Shane Arrington might just be the answer to some of their prayers. She took off for her house at a run and dialed his number without even taking off her coat.

CHAPTER

7

"Shane? It's Melanie," she said when he answered.

"Oh, hi, Mel. How's it going? Are you calling to say that you've inherited a million dollars? Or that you've found someone to take all the animals?"

Melanie crossed her fingers for luck and took a deep breath. "Not exactly," she said slowly.

"Isn't 'not exactly' usually followed by 'but'?" he asked cautiously.

This was it. There was no turning back now. "Actually it is," she said, and then plunged on in. "Not exactly, *but* I was wondering how your parents would feel about signing the adoption papers and keeping the animals at your house until we can find homes for all of them. I mean, you've said so often that your mom and dad are really cool and laid back and nothing bothers them and that they believe in love and peace and—"

"Whoa!" cried Shane. "Just a minute. Let me get this straight. You're saying that *if* we raise the money to spring the animals and *if* we can't find people to adopt them, you want *my parents* to take them all in?"

Melanie closed her eyes and crossed her fingers again. Everybody knew that Shane's parents had been hippies and that they still made the peace sign and talked about love among all people on earth. Surely they loved animals, too.

"Could you ask them?" she asked. "I mean, maybe they would. It would just be temporary until we found enough good homes, and it might save the lives of all those animals."

Shane didn't answer for a moment. Finally he sighed and said, "They aren't home right now, but even if they say it's okay, there's somebody else you're forgetting. Igor. I couldn't just bring in a bunch of strange animals without checking with him first. It would hurt his feelings."

Melanie choked back a giggle. "Okay," she said. "Talk to Igor."

Shane put down the phone and was gone for a

couple of minutes. "Hello, Melanie?" he said when he picked it up again.

"I'm still here. What did he say?"

"He isn't sure we have room. He says fifteen animals is a lot," said Shane. "But personally I think he's just afraid he won't get enough attention. Is there someone else who could keep some of them?"

Melanie bit her lower lip. "I don't know," she admitted. "We're really stuck, but maybe we could divide them up into two groups with dogs in one group and cats in another. How would he feel about taking the cats?"

Shane put down the phone and was gone again. "Igor says cats drive him nuts. They follow him around and bat at his tail as if it were a piece of string that he was dragging for them to play with."

"What about dogs?" Melanie asked, trying not to panic. She had thought Shane's parents might give them trouble, but she hadn't counted on its being *Igor*.

A moment later Shane came back on the line. "He says dogs are worse. He's nocturnal, you know, and dogs keep him awake during the day with their barking, and sometimes they even chase him."

"Oh, no," groaned Melanie. "Can't you talk to him? We really need a place to keep some of the animals. The shelter won't release them unless we can guarantee homes."

"Hold on," said Shane. "I'll try again."

This time Shane was gone forever, and Melanie was beginning to wonder if he was ever coming back when she heard him pick up the receiver.

"Okay, Mel," said Shane. "Here's the plan. Igor says that if he has to choose, it's the cats. I hope you realize that you owe him a favor now. He'll probably want you to catch some flies for him or dig him some worms."

"Yuck!" cried Melanie. "You've got to be kidding!"

"I'm not kidding," Shane assured her. "Besides, you'd better be nice to him. Igor's the only one who can convince my parents to take in the cats."

Melanie was bent over laughing when she hung up the phone. Shane had been wonderful, and she was sure that he was beginning to like her. Otherwise, he probably wouldn't have been so willing to help her out with the cats. But as much as she wanted to dream about Shane, she still had a lot to do for the second half of her plan.

She found her parents in the dining room wrapping Christmas presents.

"May I come in?" she asked timidly.

"Sure," said her mother. "Most of yours are already wrapped. We're working on Jeffy's things while he's playing at a friend's house."

Melanie glanced at the assortment of trucks and games still waiting to be wrapped. She hoped that when her parents had said *most* of her presents had been wrapped, they had meant that one would wear only a bow. A present named Rainbow.

"What is it, sweetheart?" asked her father. "Did you want to ask us something?"

Taking a deep breath, Melanie nodded. "I was just wondering if I could invite The Fabulous Five to sleep over tonight?"

Her mother was thoughtful for a moment. "I don't see why not. Do you, Larry?"

Mr. Edwards shook his head. "It's okay with me."

"Thanks," Melanie said, giving each of them a hug and bounding out of the room. She grabbed the phone and punched in the first number.

Melanie was waiting by the front door when her friends began to arrive. Jana was the first, and Melanie was glad that her parents were watching the six-o'clock news in the family room instead of sitting in the living room where they could see her friends come in.

"Come on. The coast is clear," she said, helping Jana maneuver a sleeping bag through the door that was so fat it almost got stuck. "You'd better take it upstairs to my room while I watch for the others to arrive."

Jana nodded and dragged the enormous bag up the stairs just as Katie came up the front sidewalk.

Her sleeping bag was as big as Jana's, and she tugged it up the stairs without being seen by Melanie's parents either.

By the time all of The Fabulous Five had arrived and stuffed their sleeping bags into Melanie's room, there was hardly space for the girls to squeeze in.

"Now that we've gotten them here, why did you want us to bring all these old blankets and rags hidden in our sleeping bags?" asked Christie.

Melanie listened at the door for a moment and then said, "I couldn't tell you on the phone because Mom was in the same room, but Shane and I have a plan for keeping the cats and dogs in case we can't find homes for them before Christmas Eve."

"Wow. That's great," said Beth. "What is it?"

"Shane and Igor have agreed to keep the cats at their house, and I'm going to hide the dogs in my dad's workshop behind the garage. He never goes out there this time of year, and I think I can keep my parents from finding out that the animals are there if I'm *really* careful."

"But why do you need all this stuff?" asked Katie, looking around at the assortment of rags and blankets on the floor and wrinkling her nose.

"I asked you to bring them over because the workshop isn't heated. The dogs need something to burrow into to keep warm."

"Gosh. I don't know," said Jana. "Do you really

think you can keep the dogs a secret from your parents? And how are you going to get this stuff out to the workshop without their seeing it?"

"Yes, I can keep it a secret," Melanie insisted. "And *we* are going to take this out to the workshop tonight after my parents go to sleep."

"*Oooooh,*" groaned the rest of The Fabulous Five in unison.

Sleepovers were usually a blast, but tonight was one of the longest evenings Melanie could remember. Everyone was too antsy to have any fun. Besides that, they couldn't think of anything to do. Jana tried calling Randy and Beth tried Keith's number, but neither boy was home. Then they called Mona Vaughn and talked to her about all the poor dogs and cats in the animal shelter until they were all depressed enough to cry.

"We could call kids and try to talk them into adopting an animal," suggested Beth. "Maybe Alexis Duvall would take one, or Kim Baxter."

"Naw," said Katie. "I've already talked to both of them. Alexis is allergic to animals, and Kim has a parrot named Squawker who drives her whole family crazy. I don't think she's much of a candidate for a dog or cat."

Melanie looked at her watch. It was only ten after nine. Her parents wouldn't be going to bed for a long time.

"Is anybody hungry?" she asked. Nobody was.

"Why do we have to wait until your parents go to sleep?" asked Beth. "The house will be as quiet as a tomb then. It seems to me that if we sneak out to your father's workshop now while the television is on and they're busy talking, we have a better chance of making it without being heard."

"Are you kidding?" said Christie. "What if they saw us sneaking down the stairs?"

"And carrying all this *stuff*!" cried Jana.

"I know," said Beth, rushing to Melanie's window and throwing it open. "Let's drop it out the window before we go downstairs."

"Great idea," said Melanie. She picked up an armload of rags and tossed them out into the darkness. "Come on, everybody, and help."

"What are we going to do now?" asked Christie when all the blankets and rags were gone from the room. "This is the craziest thing I've ever done in my life."

"Just follow me," instructed Melanie. "And if anybody giggles, you're dead!"

Melanie put on her jacket and mittens and listened at the door again. Behind her, the rest of The Fabulous Five were putting on their jackets, too. When everyone was ready, she opened the door and tiptoed into the hall.

"Act *casual*," she instructed as she sauntered down

the stairs. After a minute, her friends started down, too.

"Melanie? Is that you?" asked her mother from the family room. Then she stepped to the door and got a surprised look on her face. "Where on earth are you girls going at this time of night?"

Melanie gave her mother a bored look. "Oh, just out in the backyard to look at the stars," she said.

Someone choked behind her, and Melanie braced for giggling to break out. Instead, Beth pretended to cough and Christie cleared her throat.

"Did I hear you right?" asked Mrs. Edwards. "Did you say that you're going out into the backyard to look at the *stars*?"

"Sure," said Melanie, as if she had never heard such a strange question. Then she made a beeline for the back door and called back over her shoulder, "Mars is ascending into the seventh moon tonight, Mom. Didn't you know?"

As soon as the door closed behind the five of them, they couldn't hold back their giggles anymore.

"Mars is ascending into the seventh moon?" shrieked Christie between laughs. "That sounds like astrology—you know, like your horoscope—not the kind of stars you look at in the sky."

"Who cares?" said Melanie. "It worked, didn't it?"

For the next half hour the girls gathered blankets

off the grass and picked rags from out of the bushes and put them onto the workshop floor without interruption from Melanie's parents. When they were finally finished, Melanie surveyed the job with satisfaction, thinking how cozy it would be with each dog in its own little nest. Now all the animals would be saved, and there was only one major thing left to do—get the money.

CHAPTER

8

"Thirteen dollars and eighty-five cents! Is that all?" Melanie asked in disbelief. "We collected over forty dollars Friday."

"I know," said Jana. She was seated with Randy behind the collection table in the cafeteria on Monday. "The kids have been looking at the pictures Garrett took of the cats and dogs on the poster and talking about how cute they are, but most of them said they gave last week or they were broke. And *no one* signed up for a pet."

"I can't believe it either," said Katie. "Don't they care about what happens to the poor animals?"

"All I can say is, we'd better get a lot of money

65

from the newspaper ad," said Randy. "There are only five more days before Christmas Eve, and right now all we can afford to pay for is two animals."

"Well, I'm going to have to find a way to talk my mom and dad into going to look at Rainbow," said Melanie.

"Lots of luck," said Jana. "I talked to my mom and Pink last night about getting a cat, and they said no way. With both of them working and me going to school, we couldn't take care of a pet."

When Melanie got home from school, she ran into the kitchen and dropped her books on the kitchen table. "Do I have any mail?" she called.

"Who'd write to *you*?" asked Jeffy, who was sitting at the counter licking cookie batter out of a bowl.

"None of your business," said Melanie, darting her finger into the bowl and swiping some batter.

"The mail is in the family room on the TV," said Mrs. Edwards. "I think there may be a couple of letters for you. I suppose they're donations for that animal fund you're working on."

Melanie ducked out of the kitchen before her mother could ask any questions. She wasn't ready to admit that they still hadn't found homes for the dogs and cats or to take a chance on giving away her own secret plan. She grabbed the stack of envelopes and shuffled through them, taking out two that had her name on them and heading for her room.

"Don't forget your books!" called Mrs. Edwards. Melanie spun on her heel, grabbed her books, and kept going.

In her room she kicked off her shoes and jumped into the middle of her bed to open the envelopes. The first one contained a five-dollar bill wrapped in a piece of paper with a note that said, *To the save the dog fund*. It was signed, *Martha Glosner*. The shaky scrawl looked as if it had been written by a very old person. Melanie thought about Mrs. Miller, and how she loved her Duchess so much. The little dog still hadn't turned up.

The other envelope obviously had been sent by a child. It contained forty-five cents in change, which was taped to a piece of cardboard.

Melanie sat on the bed and looked at the money. Five dollars and forty-five cents. It wasn't much, but of course this was only the first day they would have received donations in the mail. With the rest of what they had collected and the money they each put into the box instead of exchanging presents, they had a little over one hundred dollars. Melanie sighed. They only had this week to raise enough money, and Christmas Eve day was getting closer and closer.

* * *

"The total now stands at one hundred seventeen dollars and sixteen cents," said Christie, as she sat at the collection table on Tuesday with her pad and pencil. Jon was sitting next to her watching her add the figures, and Shane, Randy, Melanie, and Jana were standing with them.

"Don't forget the five dollars and forty-five cents we got in the mail," reminded Melanie.

"Oh, yeah. That makes it one hundred twenty-two dollars and sixty-one cents."

"Two dollars and thirty-nine cents more and we'll have enough for five animals," said Jana.

"We're still a long way off from fifteen," said Christie, chewing on the end of her pencil. "And we've only got four days left." Worry lines etched her forehead.

"That's five more cats and dogs than we have homes for," said Shane. He was playing with two quarters he had taken from the money box. "Igor's really getting grumpy over the thought of sharing his sandbox with a bunch of cats."

"I don't blame him," said Randy. "We'd better do something fast."

"Hey, here comes Chet Miller and Jay Chisholm. Chet was in the school play with Beth, maybe he'll give something," said Jon.

"Hey, Chet. Jay," called Shane. "Step right up here and let us give you the golden opportunity of a lifetime." Shane made his voice sound as if he were a barker in a circus, trying to draw a crowd into a show. "Tell you what I'm gonna do. For the measly sum of fifty cents apiece we're going to give you a chance to win the pet of your choice. Where else can you get an offer like that?"

"That's an opportunity? It sounds more like a threat," said Chet, smiling. "My family already has a dog and two cats. If I brought another animal home, somebody would have to leave, and I think my dad would pick me."

"Well, you can at least donate fifty cents," said Jon.

Chet and Jay dug into their pockets and pulled out some change. "This is all I've got," said Jay, dropping some nickels and dimes into the box.

"There's Max McNatt. Why don't you ask him to donate?" asked Chet. "Hey, Max. Come here."

Melanie looked at Max, who was big and burly and played nose guard on the varsity football team. He wore his blond hair short and swaggered around Wakeman as if he owned the school. His round head was set right on top of his shoulders so that he reminded Melanie of a human snowman. He was blustery and scared her when she was near him, and his sister, Geena, who was in the seventh grade, was kind of wild, too.

"What do you want?" Max demanded brusquely.

"We're collecting money to save cats and dogs who

are going to be put to sleep at the animal shelter," Shane answered. "Would you like to donate?"

"Why should I?" Max responded.

Melanie stared at him with disgust. It was the sort of answer she had expected from him.

"Because you're a nice guy?" questioned Shane.

"Who told you that?"

"I heard it from the center on Georgetown's football team," Shane shot back.

Max glared at him, and Melanie saw Randy stiffen, but Shane kept his cool.

"Tell you what," said Shane. "We'll flip a coin and you can call it. If it comes up the way you say, I'll put fifty cents in. If it doesn't, you put fifty cents in."

Max's eyes narrowed as he looked at Shane. "Let me see the quarter," he growled. Shane handed it to him and he turned it over twice, looking at both sides.

Shane reached out and took it back. "That's okay, if you're afraid to take a chance." He flipped the coin and caught it.

"Heads!" shouted Max.

Shane looked at him as if he were surprised at the call. Then he slapped the quarter down in his opposite hand and held his two hands palms together and looked at Max. Slowly, he raised the top hand to reveal a quarter tails-side up.

"Darn!" said Max, reaching into his pocket and

taking out some change, which he tossed into the box before stomping off.

"That makes one hundred twenty-three dollars and eleven cents," said Shane, tossing the money he had been holding into the box, too.

Melanie stared at him, and he smiled. She could have sworn that she saw him throw in two quarters, but it had looked as if he just had one when he was flipping with Max.

"McNatt's really a sweet guy, when you get to know him," said Chet. He smiled and left.

"Max makes Ebenezer Scrooge seem nice," said Jana. "His sister Geena's in my Social Studies class, and she's always disrupting class and picking on people."

"Let's forget about them," said Christie. "Now that we're getting some money, doesn't anyone know *anyone* who wants a cat or dog?"

"What about Mrs. Miller?" asked Jana. "Did she ever find her dog, Duchess?"

"No," said Melanie. "Hey! That's an idea. If Duchess doesn't come back, maybe we can give her one."

"I don't know," said Jon, shaking his head. "Maybe she's too sad to want another dog right now."

Melanie looked at him. He might be right. "I'll ask Mom about it. She talks to Mrs. Miller a lot. Maybe she can find out."

A glimmer of an idea was starting to grow in Melanie's mind. Maybe this was just the opening she needed to get Rainbow, she thought as she headed for her afternoon classes. If she could convince her parents to go with her to the shelter to pick a new pet for Mrs. Miller, it would be the perfect opportunity to introduce them to Rainbow. It just might work, if she played it right. Maybe she would get a pet for Christmas after all.

CHAPTER

9

"Are you going to Bumpers today?" Melanie asked Katie as they were getting their books out of their lockers after school.

Katie shook her head. "I wish I could, but my sneakers are shot. Mom gave me some money this morning, and I'm going to the mall to get some new ones."

"The mall!" shrieked Melanie, slapping her forehead with the back of her hand. "Why didn't I think of that? Come on. Help me catch everybody before they leave the building."

"What are you talking about?" asked Katie. "All I said was that I was going to get new sneakers."

Melanie slammed her locker and gave Katie an exasperated look. "Don't you get it? The mall. All those shoppers with *money*. I'll bet lots of them would donate to save the animals if they had the chance."

Katie's eyes shot open as if she'd just been struck by lightning. "You're right. And *we're* going to give them a chance."

The two girls darted through the crowded hallway flagging down each of their friends before they left their lockers until they had the entire Fabulous Five together and had told them the new plan.

"I think it's terrific," said Beth. "Should we get the boys, too? I know they would help."

"There isn't time," said Jana. "I have to be home in an hour and a half."

"Besides," said Christie proudly, "this is something just for The Fabulous Five to do together."

The girls were out of breath by the time they had jogged the seven blocks to the huge downtown mall, and they exchanged smiles of victory at the bumper-to-bumper stream of cars heading into the parking garage.

"Genius, pure genius!" said Beth, patting Melanie on the back.

The interior of the mall was even more crowded than the parking garage, and the girls had to link arms to stay together in the surging crowd as they went past the picture-taking booth where Santa Claus sat, then got on the escalator up to the second level.

"How are we going to get noticed?" asked Jana.

"I brought the poster from our cafeteria table," said Christie, holding a roll of poster board out for them to see. "But I don't see anywhere to put it so that people will see it."

"I know," said Melanie. "Let's set up by the pet store in that little oasis with the indoor trees, the waterfall, and the park benches."

"Good idea," said Katie. "People shopping at the pet store ought to be especially interested in saving animals."

When they reached the spot, a pair of elderly ladies were just leaving one of the benches, and Beth grabbed it before anyone else could get there. Then the girls unrolled their poster and taped it to the backrest of the bench where it could be seen by people passing by.

"Does anyone have anything to collect the money in?" asked Jana.

Nobody did, but Melanie spotted an empty soft-drink cup floating in the fountain and retrieved it. "Here," she said, shaking off the water drops. "Okay, guys. Time to go to work."

"Excuse me, Ma'am," said Beth, stopping a plump woman coming out of the pet store. She was carrying a cat's clawing post decorated with a big red ribbon. "Wouldn't you like to help save the lives of fifteen dogs and cats that the local animal shelter is going to put to sleep on Christmas Eve?"

The lady looked startled. "Christmas Eve? Oh, my."

"That's right," piped up Melanie. "It costs twenty-five dollars apiece to adopt the animals, and we're trying to raise enough money to adopt all of them."

The lady gave a breathless little sigh and set down the clawing post. Then she dug into her purse and pulled out a dollar bill. "Here," she said. "Good luck."

Melanie and Beth looked at each other in wide-eyed disbelief. "Why didn't we think of this before?" Melanie burst out. "It's a snap."

"What's this about animals being put to sleep?"

The girls looked up to see a man standing beside them in jeans and a ski jacket, holding the hands of two snowsuited toddlers.

"That's right," said Christie. "The animal shelter is overcrowded and they have no choice."

"Well, we certainly want to do something about that, don't we, kids?"

The two children nodded their heads vigorously. Then the man handed each of them a quarter and instructed them to drop it into the cup.

"Wow!" cried Beth. "This is what I call Christmas!"

"Just a moment, young ladies." The voice that spoke this time did not sound friendly, and the girls turned to see a mall security guard with his arms folded across his chest, frowning at them. "I'd like to know what you think you're doing?"

"We're . . . um . . ." Melanie stammered.

"We're collecting money to save the lives of fifteen dogs and cats at the animal shelter," spoke up Katie.

"And of course *you know* that soliciting in the mall without a permit is against the law," the guard said sternly. "There are signs posted all over the mall," he added, pointing to a large sign beside the door to the pet store that said: ABSOLUTELY NO SOLICITING IN THE MALL.

Melanie cringed. She had been in the mall thousands of times, but this was the first time she had ever seen the sign.

"Gosh, Officer. We're sorry," she said. "We didn't realize we were breaking the law. We're only trying to help the animals."

The officer's expression softened a little. "The correct procedure is to go to the main office of the mall on the first floor and fill out a request for a permit. The office will review it, check your references, and let you know in a few days."

Melanie's shoulders slumped. "Thanks," she said, "but we don't have a few days."

The girls rolled up their poster again and headed for the exit, saying good-bye to Katie, who still had to shop for sneakers.

"I guess we'll just have to think of something else," said Jana.

Melanie nodded and then brightened. "Well, at least we got another dollar and fifty cents."

"Wow! Look at all the mail Melanie's got." Jeffy grabbed for the envelopes Melanie had in her hands a little while later, and she jerked them away.

"Leave me alone, squirt. These are donations." She thumbed through them, counting. "Seven. That's more like it," she said with a smile.

"You're keeping track of the money you're getting, aren't you?" asked her mother.

"We sure are," Melanie answered, heading for her room. "Christie's our accountant," she called over her shoulder.

"Oh, that reminds me," her mother called after her. "Mona Vaughn called to say that the shelter will give you a fifty-dollar discount. Congratulations."

"Whoopee!" Melanie sang to herself as she raced into her room. After the disastrous trip to the mall, she needed cheering up. "And I'll bet there's fifty dollars here." She dropped the envelopes on her desk and tore one open. It contained five dollars. She laid it on the corner of her desk and put the accompanying letter aside.

The rest of the envelopes had an assortment of money from two to ten dollars. The total was thirty-three dollars.

Melanie held the stack of money against her cheek. It wasn't fifty dollars, but it was a lot more than the five dollars and forty-five cents they had gotten in the mail the day before. It was enough for one and a half animals, and if she got even more tomorrow and the next day, they had a chance to get the three hundred and twenty-five dollars they needed now with the fifty-dollar discount from the shelter.

She arranged the letters that had come with the money in a neat stack to look at later. I'll call Christie right away, she thought, getting up. She can tell me what the new total is and we can count dogs and cats. When Melanie came into the living room, she found her mother with Mrs. Miller.

"Sit down, Clare, and tell us what's wrong." Mrs. Edwards was holding Mrs. Miller's arm and helping her into a chair. Melanie had been so busy with the money she hadn't heard the doorbell chime. Mrs. Miller's eyes were red, as if she had been crying, and she was holding a scrap of paper in her hand.

"I've just received a call from Mrs. Mertz on Sherwood Street," she said in a shaky voice as she wiped her eyes with a crumpled tissue.

"There, there," said Melanie's mother, patting her hand. "Can we get you a glass of water or something?" Mrs. Miller waved her hand to reject the offer.

"What did Mrs. Mertz say?" asked Mrs. Edwards.

Mrs. Miller looked up at her. Her eyes were brimming with tears. "They said they found the body of a little Pomeranian dog that had a tag saying its name was Duchess, and my telephone number was on it."

"Way over on Sherwood?" Melanie said in disbelief. "How could she have gotten way over there?"

Mrs. Miller shook her head. "They said it looked as if she had been run over."

"Oh, my," said Melanie's mother. "Did they give you their address?"

Mrs. Miller held up the paper she had been holding, and Mrs. Edwards took it.

After she read it, she handed it to Melanie. "Your father's down in the basement. Go tell him what's happened, and ask him if he'll go get Duchess. Tell him to take a box along."

Melanie went with her father to get Duchess. When they returned, he got a shovel, and they scraped the snow away and buried the little box with

the body in it in the corner of Mrs. Miller's backyard.

"Go get your mother and Clare," said Mr. Edwards. "We'll show them where Duchess is buried."

Melanie did as she was told, but before she followed them back to Mrs. Miller's yard, she ran into
the family room and took a red carnation from a
vase.

When she joined the others at the small grave site,
she handed the carnation to Mrs. Miller. The older
lady smiled at her and laid in on the little mound of
earth.

CHAPTER

10

"That was so sad," said Melanie at the dinner table that night. "Mrs. Miller really took it hard."

"Yes, she did," her mother agreed. "She had Duchess for a long time. The little dog was like a baby to her. A lot of older people need animals as companions. They give them something to care for that can return their affection."

"I was thinking," said Melanie. "Would it be too soon to give her another dog?"

Her mother looked at her with raised eyebrows.

"My friends and I have enough money to buy four or five dogs or cats, and it just seems like a good idea

THE CHRISTMAS COUNTDOWN 83

to give one to her." Melanie hurriedly added, "But we wouldn't do it unless Mrs. Miller wanted one."

"That's very thoughtful, Melanie," said her mother.

"Do you think you could talk to her and see how she feels about it?" asked Melanie. "We're going to have some super dogs and cats. Maybe she'd rather have a cat this time."

"It might be a little too early for her to take either, sweetheart, but if it seems right, I'll talk to her."

Later in her room, Melanie sat staring at her open English book, absentmindedly drawing Santa Clauses in her notebook. It had all seemed so simple when she had thought up the idea of saving the animals. There were all those beautiful kittens and puppies and older animals. All Melanie and her friends needed was money and people to take them. How could anyone resist giving money to save such sweet animals or not want to give a home to one of them?

She looked at the picture of herself and Mona with Rainbow that she had thumbtacked over her desk. It seemed impossible that someone wouldn't want Rainbow. She was so loving and trusting. Melanie moved her fingers across the photo. She could almost feel the fine hair covering the dog's gorgeous head. She bit her lip to hold back the tears. In a way she knew how Mrs. Miller felt.

She sighed and thought about her and Shane's plan to keep the animals if Christmas Eve came before they found homes for them. It was a crazy plan, and she had avoided even thinking about it, hoping instead that people who wanted the pets really would come forward. But what if no one did? What if she was stuck with eight or nine dogs hidden in her father's workshop? How would she feed them? Or let them out to go to the bathroom? What had she been thinking about anyway?

Melanie stood up and began pacing around her room. "There has to be a better way to publicize this," she said out loud. "Just putting an ad in the newspaper isn't enough. We've got to get the word out to everyone in town that we need homes for these animals."

Of course there's television, she thought, but how . . . The idea hit her like an avalanche. Jon Smith could get them on television. His parents were Marge Whitworth and Chip Smith, local television personalities. His mother even anchored the evening news program. All they would have to do was convince her that their project was newsworthy and maybe, just *maybe*, she would put it on the air. Melanie dashed downstairs and called Jon on the phone.

"She'll go for it," Jon shouted when he had heard

her idea. "I know she will. Let me talk to her and call you back."

Half an hour later the phone rang. It was Jon. "She loved it. She said to be at the shelter tomorrow after school, and she'll get a camera crew there from the station. She even said that we'll make the six-o'clock news."

Melanie was ecstatic. She called everyone she could think of and told them the news.

The next afternoon spirits were high as at least twenty kids tramped to the shelter behind The Fabulous Five, Mona, and the boys. Some carried hand-lettered signs saying things such as, "Save the animals!" and "Don't let innocent dogs and cats die at Christmas!"

When they arrived at the animal shelter, Mrs. Graham was all flustered.

"Oh, my gosh!" cried Melanie. "She's the one person I forgot to call."

"It's okay," Mrs. Graham assured her. "In fact, it's wonderful."

Just then Marge Whitworth rushed forward and began shouting instructions. "Okay, kids. Listen up. I want a dozen volunteers to hold the animals for the camera."

Every hand shot up, but Jon went to her and whispered something in her ear.

"Okay," she said. "The boys and girls who've been working to raise money should come forward."

Melanie couldn't suppress a grin as The Fabulous Five, Mona, Matt, Scott, Shane, Tony, Keith, and Jon made their way through the crowd. Then she spied Randy hanging back. Why hadn't he stepped up with the rest of them? Melanie wondered. He had helped as much as anybody. Then she realized why Randy hadn't moved. He would make number thirteen, and Ms. Whitworth had said she needed twelve volunteers.

Jon noticed it, too, and whispered to his mother again, and she motioned Randy forward with the others.

Ms. Whitworth arranged them in a semicircle facing the camera, and when it started to roll, Charles handed each of them one of the dogs or cats from the cages. Each animal was leashed, and Charles cautioned them to hold on to the leashes for dear life. Then Marge Whitworth stepped in front of the group, faced the camera, and began speaking into her microphone.

"Ladies and gentlemen, I'm here at the local animal shelter today to bring you the story of a dedicated group of students from Wakeman Junior High who are working hard to save the lives of fifteen dogs and cats, victims of overcrowding at the shelter, who are doomed to die on Christmas Eve."

Melanie was holding Rainbow, and she listened to Jon's mother and stroked the dog's head at the same time. She could feel Rainbow's little heart beating furiously, and she longed to whisper to her that everything would be all right.

"With only three days left and only halfway to their goal of three hundred . . ."

Suddenly the Labrador retriever Matt was holding broke loose and lunged for the long-haired gray cat in Christie's arms. Christie screamed, dropping the cat, and pandemonium broke out as a boxer and a Border collie took off in opposite directions, getting tangled up in each other's leashes, and a calico cat yowled and swiped a black poodle across the nose. What happened after that was anyone's guess, Melanie thought later. Dogs were barking, kids were screeching, and cats were hissing and arching their backs, and Rainbow snuggled deeper into Melanie's arms.

The only sound heard over the melee was Marge Whitworth's strong voice calling, *"CUT!"*

CHAPTER

11

*O*nce order was restored and all the animals were back in their cages, Melanie approached Marge Whitworth, who was talking to her camera crew.

"I guess you won't be able to use our story now, will you?" she asked.

The anchorwoman threw back her head and laughed. "Of course I will. In fact, I'll use it on both the six- and eleven-o'clock news. If that wild scene doesn't point up the need for people to help out the shelter, nothing will."

Melanie passed on the good news to the rest of the kids, who were congregated outside. Then she hurried home, feeling exuberant. They were going to get the publicity they needed after all. Now surely the money would come pouring in as well as offers for homes for some of the animals.

"Guess what!" she called as she raced into her house and sailed into the kitchen. "We're going to be on the news at both six and eleven."

"Catch your breath," said her mother, "and speak more slowly. What are you saying?"

Melanie gasped and then went on to tell her mother about the dog-and-cat fight during the taping of the TV spot. "But Marge Whitworth says she's going to run it anyway. She says it will get more attention than if the animals had all behaved."

"That's great, sweetheart. We'll be sure to watch. In fact, we'll tape it on the VCR if you'd like."

Melanie nodded and had started up to her room when her mother called to her.

"I thought you'd like to know that I went over to Mrs. Miller's today, and on top of everything else that's happened to her, the poor soul twisted her ankle going down her stairs. The Visiting Nurses Association is sending a nurse's aide over to help her with her cooking and chores for a couple of days. I told Mrs. Crenshaw, the nurse's aide, that I'd look in on Clare this evening. You know, Melanie, I think your idea of getting her another dog to take her mind off Duchess might just be what she needs. Since Clare lives alone, she doesn't have anything else to occupy her mind, and now with the bad ankle, she's awfully blue. This is not going to be a good Christmas for her."

Melanie spun around and hugged herself for joy. This was exactly the opportunity she had been waiting for to put her plan about Rainbow in action. "Can we go look for a pet for her this evening after we watch the six-o'clock news? Mona said the shelter is open until eight o'clock so people can go after work."

"I don't see why not," said her mother, and Melanie thought she would die from relief.

When her father got home, Melanie told him about the television taping at the shelter. He helped her set the VCR so that they could get a permanent copy of her television debut, and the whole family gathered around the set as the news came on.

Marge Whitworth opened the broadcast with a few stories of national interest. Then she talked about a robbery on the east side of town. Jeffy was getting fidgety, and Melanie could hardly sit still herself. Finally the big moment arrived.

"In other news around town, I spent some time at our local animal shelter this afternoon filming a very special Christmas project," said Ms. Whitworth.

Her face disappeared from the screen for an instant, and when it reappeared, she was in the animal

THE CHRISTMAS COUNTDOWN 91

shelter, standing in front of all the kids and their animals.

"This is it!" shrieked Melanie.

Jeffy jumped off his stool and ran to the television, jabbing the screen with his finger. "There you are! Melanie, you're on TV!"

"That's what I told you, silly," said Melanie.

She motioned him to be quiet as the anchorwoman began speaking. "Ladies and gentlemen, I'm here at the local animal shelter today . . ."

Melanie sat spellbound watching herself and her friends on television. But as much fun as that was, it was Rainbow whom she couldn't take her eyes off of. The little dog was so gentle, even when the others went wild, and the way she snuggled close made tears of longing come to Melanie's eyes.

Everyone was laughing like crazy by the time the segment was over.

"That was an awfully nice dog you were holding," said her mother. "In fact, I'd say it was the pick of the bunch."

Melanie wanted to grab her mother and hug her, but she didn't dare. It was critical that she didn't blow her chances of getting Rainbow now, just when it was time for her parents to meet the dog in person.

A few minutes later the family got into the car for

the drive to the shelter, but before she left the house, Melanie hurried to her room for the one special thing she wanted to take along.

"Wow!" said Jeffy as they walked into the animal shelter. "Look at all the cages. And there are cats and dogs in all of them." He ran forward and dropped to his knees in front of one cage, his hands gripping the wire bars. The yellow cocker spaniel inside licked his nose, making Jeffy giggle.

Besides the garland along the top of the cages, the shelter employees had added brightly colored bows to the cage doors. The room looked cheerful, and Mrs. Graham was showing animals to two other families. A little girl was holding a dachshund that wiggled in her arms until Melanie thought she might drop it. The other family had a cat with a pushed-in face that made it look as if it were crabby.

"See," said Melanie, pulling her mother by the hand to the cages. "Aren't they all just gorgeous?" She watched her mother's face closely to see her reaction. She knew that this would be her last chance to change her parents' minds about getting a pet.

Mr. Edwards followed as they walked along the rows looking at the animals. The sternness had melted out of her mother's eyes as she looked at the animals, and Melanie's heart quickened. Was her mother's resolve not to get a dog weakening?

"Look at this little dog," said Melanie, pointing to a cage that contained the small white dog that Garrett had photographed on Saturday. It looked more like the end of her mother's dust mop than an animal.

Mrs. Edwards stuck her finger into the cage. The black button nose sniffed at it and then its little pink tongue flicked out and licked it. Mrs. Edwards smiled the way Melanie remembered her smiling when she held Jeffy when he was a baby.

"Isn't he sweet," her mother cooed.

"I'll bet Mrs. Miller would like a dog like that," said Melanie. "He's not very big and he would be easy to take care of."

"Maybe so," her mother answered.

"Look! Look!" squealed Jeffy. A kitten had its paw stretched out as far as it could reach and was swatting at him. Jeffy swatted back gently with his forefinger.

"Can we get one? Oh, can we, please?" he pleaded.

"We're here to look for a dog for Mrs. Miller, not for us," said Mrs. Edwards.

"Daddy talks about the dogs he had when he was little," said Jeffy. "Why can't we have one?"

Mrs. Edwards looked at her husband, her eyes pleading for help. He had a noncommittal half-smile on his face and didn't say a word.

Now's the time if it ever will be, Melanie thought. "Let me show you someone special." She gripped her mother's and father's hands and pulled them toward the end of the row of cages. Jeffy followed, trying to look in all directions at once.

Rainbow raised her head as they approached her cage and wagged her tail in greeting. Melanie thought she could see recognition in the big brown eyes. She wondered if the dog knew that she was trying hard to help.

"Hello, Melanie." Mrs. Graham had left the other people. "Are you here to visit your friend?"

"Yes, Ma'am. Can we let her out?"

"I don't know if that's necessary," said Mrs. Edwards.

"Surely. It's no problem at all," said Mrs. Graham. "Here, let me do it." She opened the door and then returned to the other people.

Rainbow looked at them tentatively, as if she were surprised at the door's being open. Then she came out wagging her tail and sat pressing her shoulder against Melanie.

"Look! She's smiling," said Jeffy. "I didn't know dogs could smile."

"Some dogs do," said his father. "It's their way of showing they're glad to see you."

Melanie caught the look of hopelessness in her mother's eyes and knew she was breaking. She stroked Rainbow's silken sides as Jeffy held her head and talked to her.

As the family hovered around the dog, Melanie put the last part of her plan into action. She reached into her pocket and pulled out a big Christmas bow with a ribbon attached that she had brought especially for Rainbow. She carefully put the bow on the back of Rainbow's neck and tied the ribbon under her chin. She looked beautiful.

"Rainbow is one of the animals that will be put to sleep on Christmas Eve if someone doesn't take her," Melanie said quietly. She heard her mother sigh. It was the same sigh Melanie had heard her make when she had given in on other things. "Can we take her when we come to get the animals? It won't cost us anything, and Jeffy and I will take care of her. We promise."

"Yeah, we promise!" shouted Jeffy, jumping up and down in his excitement.

Mrs. Edwards stood there while her family stared at her, waiting for her next words. She shrugged. "I suppose a grown dog wouldn't be as much trouble to train as a puppy. But we'll put a schedule on the refrigerator showing whose week it is to take care of her," she added sternly. Mrs. Edwards reached down and patted Rainbow on the head, and the dog leaned against her.

Just then Mrs. Graham walked up to them again. "Oh, Melanie. You'll be glad to hear that Rainbow will be getting a home. Just before you got here, a family came in who had seen her on the six-o'clock news. They're going to come back in the morning to sign the adoption papers and take her home."

Melanie was thunderstruck. She couldn't even answer Mrs. Graham. All she could do was hug Rainbow tightly while the little dog licked the tears off her cheeks.

CHAPTER

12

*M*elanie watched numbly as her parents paid for the little white dog, whose name turned out to be Jo-Jo, and filled out all the adoption papers stating that they would guarantee that he would be taken care of or they would return him to the animal shelter. She knew she should be glad that Mrs. Miller was getting a new friend and that Jo-Jo was getting a home, but her heart was breaking over Rainbow.

Why had that other family had to watch TV tonight? And why couldn't they have picked some other dog besides Rainbow? Even though her parents had been sympathetic, and her mother had even said she could look for another dog after Christmas,

Melanie knew that Rainbow was the only dog in the world for her.

After they got home from the shelter, Melanie and Jeffy found a large cardboard box and cut the sides down on it. Then they dug through the off-season closet in the garage and found an old set of curtains that their mother said they could use for bedding.

They put Jo-Jo into the box and gave him some of the food that Mrs. Graham had given them to carry them over. The family agreed that it was too late to take him over to Mrs. Miller that night and that they would give him to her the next evening.

After Jo-Jo was settled, Melanie slipped on her jacket again and tiptoed out to the workshop. She stepped inside and flipped on the light switch, looking down at the piles of blankets and rags her friends had helped her assemble for the homeless dogs. How could she possibly take care of the other animals when Rainbow would be with someone else? Why did I start this whole thing in the first place? she asked herself. I wouldn't have, she thought angrily, if I had known how much it was going to hurt.

Melanie dreaded going to school on Thursday morning, but when she got there she noticed a large crowd gathered by the fence where The Fabulous Five stood every morning. Besides her friends, there were the boys and Mona Vaughn. Not only that, they were all talking at the same time.

"There she is!" shouted Jana when she saw Melanie coming toward them.

"It's fantastic," cried Christie. "Everyone saw us on TV last night, and lots of kids have come up and contributed already this morning."

Melanie tried to smile, but she couldn't.

"What's wrong?" asked Jana, stepping forward and taking Melanie's hand.

Quietly Melanie told them about Rainbow. Nobody said a word for a moment, and even though Melanie knew that her friends were all sympathizing with her, the ache in her heart would not go away. Finally she looked up and said, "There is some good news, though. Mrs. Miller is going to get Jo-Jo, the little white dog in one of Garrett's pictures. We're taking him to her tonight."

"MELANIE!" Jeffy came running down the hall, his feet pounding like a herd of football players. "Melanie! Dad's home!" he shouted as he hurtled into her room. "It's time to take Jo-Jo to Mrs. Miller."

"I heard you the first time you yelled! I'm coming."

When Melanie got to the kitchen, Jeffy was jumping up and down trying to hurry his father. Mrs. Edwards was smiling and taking off her apron.

"Give me a chance to get my coat off at least," said Mr. Edwards.

"I'll take your coat to your room," Jeffy volunteered.

Melanie hadn't seen him so excited since last Christmas when he got his first video game. She knew her father's coat would end up wadded on the bed, if not on the floor. Jeffy was too wound up to even think about hanging it up.

When everyone was reassembled in the kitchen, Mrs. Edwards said, "I found a box that I think Jo-Jo will fit in nicely, and we can surprise Clare by letting her open it. Melanie, you and Jeffy get him, and I'll get the box."

"I can get him by myself," said Jeffy, scampering toward the garage door.

"Jeffy!" His father's commanding voice brought him to a screeching halt. "Take it easy, Son. I know you're excited, but let Melanie help. This is a family project, you know."

Melanie sighed. She didn't really feel like helping. It was going to take all her energy to act happy when they gave Jo-Jo to Mrs. Miller.

The little white dog fit perfectly in the box. The last thing Melanie saw was its little black eyes looking questioningly up as the lid was closed over it. Mrs. Edwards put a stick-on Christmas bow on top.

Melanie and Jeffy each carried one side of the package on the way over to Mrs. Miller's. It wasn't heavy, and Jeffy could have carried it by himself, but she was sure he'd drop it if he did. Melanie was surprised when a lady in a blue uniform answered the door.

"Hello," she said cheerfully. "Come on in. I was just finishing up my visit with Mrs. Miller." She stood back as the Edwards family trooped in. Melanie and Jeffy came last, carrying the box between them as if they were two wise men bringing a gift.

"This is my husband, Larry, my daughter, Melanie, and my son, Jeffy," said Mrs. Edwards. "This is Mrs. Crenshaw," she said to her family. "She's the nurse's aide I mentioned who is taking care of Clare for a few days because of her ankle."

Mrs. Miller was sitting in a big overstuffed chair by the window with her wrapped ankle on a footstool. Her face brightened slightly when she saw the Edwards family, but she still looked sad and tired. Melanie noticed that Mrs. Miller hadn't even bothered putting up a Christmas tree this year. She knew it was because of losing Duchess, and she suddenly knew how Mrs. Miller felt.

"Hello, Clare," said Mrs. Edwards in her most cheerful voice. Melanie recognized it as the voice her mother reserved for company or when Melanie brought home an A on her report card. "How are you feeling today?"

"Fine," Mrs. Miller said with obvious effort.

"She's doing really well," said Mrs. Crenshaw, who was putting on her coat to leave.

"Well, we've brought you something special that might help cheer you up," said Mr. Edwards. He and Mrs. Edwards stepped back to let Melanie and Jeffy come forward with their present. They put the box down on the footstool in front of her chair.

"MERRY CHRISTMAS!" they all yelled in unison.

"My, what's this?" Mrs. Miller asked. Faint scratching noises came from inside, and she raised her eyebrows questioningly.

"Be careful when you open it," Jeffy said importantly.

Mrs. Miller removed the bow and her fingers fumbled at the lid. Melanie watched her face intently, wondering how she would feel when she saw Jo-Jo.

Finally, Mrs. Miller pulled the lid back and looked inside. Her face was expressionless for a moment, and then Melanie heard a small whimper, and

Jo-Jo's white head popped up like a jack-in-the-box, and he licked Mrs. Miller on the nose.

Melanie's eyes brimmed with tears when the look on Mrs. Miller's face turned from astonishment to one of warmth as she looked at the furry little creature. She took Jo-Jo and held him against her chest. The dog squirmed in her arms and licked her cheek, all the while its tail whipped back and forth like a furry little switch.

Maybe I shouldn't forget about all the other animals just because I can't have Rainbow, Melanie thought. She'll have a good home, and all the others need good homes, too. Just like Jo-Jo.

"Well, isn't that a nice present, Clare?" Mrs. Crenshaw broke into the moment.

"His name's Jo-Jo!" blurted out Jeffy. "And if you need someone to walk him, I'll do it."

Mrs. Miller smiled at him over Jo-Jo's shaggy white back.

Melanie's mother moved closer, and Jeffy reached out to pat the dog's back.

"I think Jo-Jo's exactly what Mrs. Miller needed," whispered Mrs. Crenshaw to Melanie and her father. "She has been grieving over the loss of Duchess and needed *something* to take her mind off it. So many elderly people would benefit from the companionship of pets. Their children are grown and have work and families of their own to take care of and just can't spend the time with them." They moved toward the front door as she talked.

"Most elderly people aren't able to work or get out of the house because of their physical condition, and they spend an awful lot of time alone with their memories. Pets give them something to care about and take care of. It makes them feel that they're still useful. In fact, I've read that elderly people who have pets live longer than those who don't. Many nursing homes are starting to bring pets in to help the elderly. They even provide protection."

"Protection?" Jeffy had followed them into the foyer.

"Yes. You know a dog can hear a lot of things that even you and I can't. They alert the elderly that someone may be at the door, and most burglars won't go into a home where there's a barking dog. It's too bad that all elderly people can't all have someone like Jo-Jo."

Melanie's mind snapped to attention. "Why don't they all have pets?" she asked.

"Some are too disabled to take care of them, but many just can't afford them. There are all the shots and the license to pay for besides the cost of the animal itself."

"Do you know a lot of elderly people who would like a pet?" asked Melanie.

"Why, yes, I know a few. I meet them in my work, just as I met Mrs. Miller. You see, as an aide for the Visiting Nurses Association, it's my job to visit the homes of elderly and disabled people and help them in any way I can. There are a few of my people who would benefit from having a friend like Jo-Jo."

"Do you know maybe . . . thirteen?" Melanie persisted. She hoped her voice didn't sound too excited.

Mrs. Crenshaw looked at her inquisitively. "Thirteen? I don't know that many personally, but I'm sure that if I asked the other nurse's aides and visiting nurses I work with, we could come up with that many easily."

Melanie felt herself almost losing control as the excitement built up in her. She started bouncing up and down on her toes and wanted to hug Mrs. Crenshaw. Instead, she asked, "Could you get a list of their names and addresses?"

"I guess I could," answered Mrs. Crenshaw. "But why?"

"Because I've got *thirteen* more pets just like Jo-Jo looking for someone to give them a home! *And they're all free!*"

CHAPTER

13

*M*elanie could scarcely believe how things were turning out. What had started out as an idea to simply save some homeless animals from being put to sleep on Christmas Eve day had grown into a super way to bring love and companionship to a group of elderly people. It was going to be the best Christmas ever. Except for Rainbow, she thought wistfully. Someone would have the dog, but it wouldn't be she.

Melanie couldn't wait to tell everyone about their good luck, but she decided to let them know all at one time. So she telephoned each of the kids who had worked on the pet project and told them to *defi-*

nitely be by the fence before school in the morning because she had *big* news.

"Okay. What's the big news?" asked Shane on Friday morning when everyone was assembled by the fence.

"Yeah," said Keith. "This had better be good. I need to get in and review my history notes for a test."

"*It is big news*," said Melanie, pausing for effect. And then she told them about her conversation with Mrs. Crenshaw and that she had told Melanie that she would talk to the other nurse's aides and visiting nurses and get the names of elderly people who would like to have pets and whether each one would prefer a cat or a dog. She was going to call Melanie after work that evening. "Then all we have to do is make arrangements to call the people who want pets to be sure they'll be home and then get the animals from the shelter on Christmas Eve day and deliver them."

"Wow!" said Randy. "That's awesome!"

"Right on!" shouted Matt as he hugged Mona.

"I can't wait to tell Igor," said Shane. "His tail curls up every time I mention those cats sleeping in his box."

Everyone cheered and congratulated Melanie.

"It looks as if we've done it," said Jon.

"Not until we've collected that last fifty-one dollars and seventy-seven cents," said Christie. "Until we get that, there will still be *two* animals left at the shelter that might be put to sleep."

"One," Melanie corrected her. "Don't forget Rainbow. She's already been adopted." Then, sighing, she added, "That takes the amount we need down to twenty-six dollars and seventy-seven cents."

"We've still got today and tomorrow to get the money," said Katie, giving Melanie's hand a sympathetic squeeze.

"How much did we collect at lunchtime today?" asked Tony. They were all seated in the corner booth at Bumpers.

"Three dollars and a dime," said Christie.

"Is that all?" asked Randy.

"That's it," Christie assured him.

"And there was only one contribution in the mail, and it was five dollars," said Melanie. "It was from someone who had sent in money before, too. A Mrs. Glosner." She had remembered the shaky handwriting from before.

"Gee, we still need over eighteen dollars," said Mona.

"All the kids are tapped out," said Keith. "They've given all their extra allowance and lunch money."

"I guess we're just going to have to hit our parents up again," said Scott.

"I've gotten everything I can get out of mine," said Matt.

"Well, we've still got tomorrow," said Melanie.

"But it's Saturday," Katie said dejectedly.

"We're so close," insisted Jana. "We can't leave any of the animals there to be put to sleep."

"Yeah. And I keep thinking about what you said about elderly people needing pets for companions," said Beth. "You know, I don't think we should quit after we've paid for these animals and given them to people who need them. There are more of both, and it seems like a shame that we can't get them together."

"I agree," said Katie.

Melanie felt tingly all over. She knew where the conversation was headed, and she was thrilled. "Me, too. It doesn't *have* to be the Christmas season to help. Why don't we all agree to continue saving money all through the year to buy cats and dogs to give to people who need them?"

"I second that motion," said Shane, smiling at her.

"Well, for now, assume that we'll have the money for all thirteen cats and dogs," Melanie said, getting back to business. "Who can get their parents to deliver the animals?"

"I can!" said Mona, waving her hand.

"There are thirteen animals and sixteen of us," said Christie. "That means that some of us can be partners and deliver them together. That way no one will be left out."

"That's a good idea," Melanie said. "Shane and I will be partners, and we'll even deliver two. Who else wants to be partners?"

"That sounds great!" said Jana. "Randy and I can deliver two, also."

The others began pairing up and deciding how many animals they could take. In spite of everyone's talking at once, by the time they were ready to leave Bumpers, every single animal had a ride to its new home.

"Melanie! Telephone!" Jeffy shrieked in her ear.

Melanie was barely able to uncross her eyes by the time she picked up the phone.

It was Mrs. Crenshaw. "I've got the list of names for you, Melanie. In fact, I've got more than the thirteen that you asked for."

"That's great, Mrs. Crenshaw," Melanie said. "We're going to try and get more donations for animals after Christmas, too. We hope to get more pets for the elderly."

"This is a wonderful thing you kids are doing,

Melanie. You don't know how much happiness you're going to bring to thirteen old people on Christmas Eve."

Suddenly a sad feeling came over Melanie. "I'm not sure that we're going to have the money to give pets to all thirteen. We've only collected enough for twelve animals so far."

"Oh? Well, have I got good news for you," said Mrs. Crenshaw cheerfully. "The aides and nurses that I talked to were so impressed with what you are doing that they all wanted to contribute. Would eighty-five dollars help you out? That's how much they donated."

Melanie looked at the telephone she held in her hand. Eighty-five dollars? *That would be more than enough.* They could even adopt an extra pet for that and have some left over to build their savings for more.

"Oh, Mrs. Crenshaw. Thank you! Thank you! Thank you!" exclaimed Melanie. "I love you."

Mrs. Crenshaw laughed and told Melanie that rather than reading the list of names over the phone, she would stop by on her way home and drop it and the money off.

Melanie was dancing when she went into the kitchen to tell her mother the news.

CHAPTER

14

*M*elanie couldn't believe the size of the crowd in front of the animal shelter. It was four o'clock on Christmas Eve afternoon and there were cars lined up all the way down the block. The Edwardses had been the first to arrive so their car was parked right in front of the shelter. Beth Barry's family's van was parked right behind it, and Shane's father's orange Volkswagen with the flowers and the butterflies painted on the sides was stopped, letting Shane out. Inside, the foyer was crowded with the kids and their parents.

"All right, everyone," Mrs. Graham said loudly so she could be heard. "I'll have Charles bring the animals in one at a time. I'd appreciate it if the family who is going to be responsible for it will come forward and sign a release paper. Remember, I need to have *all* the signed adoption papers back here by the end of the next week."

Charles had exchanged his baseball cap for a red Santa's hat, and he brought the Labrador retriever out first.

"He's ours!" yelled Keith, and he, Beth, and her parents made their way through the people to get him and complete the paperwork.

As Charles brought the animals out one by one, Melanie felt a swelling of pride in her chest. Each of the dogs pranced out excitedly, as if they knew they were going to a *real* home. The kittens and cats seemed more afraid, but they relaxed once they were safely in the arms of the boy or girl who reached out to take them. This could be the most exciting thing I've ever done, Melanie thought.

"We've had several donations from people who saw the television coverage," said Mrs. Graham to Melanie. "And three people called to say they'd stop by later today to see if we had any dogs left for adoption. Thanks to you boys and girls, the animal shelter may be empty for Christmas."

Melanie and Shane exchanged thumbs-up and smiles.

When Charles brought out the poodle named

Jocko, Melanie said, "That one is for us." One of the names on the list of the elderly had been familiar to her, and she thought the poodle might just be the right pet for that person. Mrs. Martha Glosner must be a special person because she had donated twice to their fund by mail.

When Melanie had called her on the phone to tell her she would be bringing her a little friend, Mrs. Glosner had been overjoyed. She said she loved animals but couldn't afford one herself, and her donations had been her way of helping out as much as she could.

After the poodle, the Edwardses and Shane claimed possession of the Persian cat with the pushed-in face. While her father signed the release and got the adoption papers for the animals, Melanie glanced back to the door to the room where the animals were, thinking about Rainbow. I wonder if her new family has picked her up yet? she thought.

"There," said Mrs. Graham as Melanie's father signed the last paper. "I believe that takes care of all the animals."

"No, Ma'am," said Charles. "You're forgetting the one that didn't get adopted because the people changed their minds."

"What?" said Melanie. Her heart was racing. "Which animal didn't get adopted?"

"Oh, yes," said Mrs. Graham. "I did forget,

didn't I?" Turning to Melanie, she said. "It's your little friend, Rainbow. The family decided not to take her when they found out about her condition."

"Her condition?" queried Mrs. Edwards, who had come up to stand beside Melanie when Rainbow's name was mentioned.

"Didn't you know? I'm so sorry, I thought you did," said Mrs. Graham. Rainbow is, uh . . . she's going to be a mother. I guess it was hard to tell when she was just in her cage or sitting down."

Melanie's heart leapt. Rainbow was still there! That meant she still needed a home!

"Do you mean she's going to have puppies?" Mrs. Edwards asked, her eyes wide and her mouth dropping open.

"I think that's usually what it means when dogs are going to be mothers, Kathy," said Mr. Edwards, chuckling.

"Oh, Mom. You said we could have her before we knew the other family might take her. We can't desert her now," Melanie pleaded, bouncing up and down on her tiptoes. "Oh, please! She needs us more than ever."

Mrs. Edwards turned and looked at her daughter, and Melanie had never seen a more helpless look on her mother's face. "But . . ." she started to say. Then she shrugged and ruffled Melanie's hair. "Bring her out," she said softly.

*　*　*

Melanie sat amidst the piles of wrapping paper and boxes on Christmas morning. The new sweater and skirt she had gotten from her parents were folded neatly on the arm of the couch, the things her grand-parents had sent her were on the table in front of her, and she had the cassette tape that Jeffy had given her in her hand. She was debating whether she wanted to get up and play it or just bask in the pleasure of thinking about Christmas Eve.

The Edwardses and Shane had delivered the poo-dle to Mrs. Glosner, who lived in the poorer section of town. She was widowed, just like Mrs. Miller, and hugged the poodle nearly the whole time they were with her. The poodle seemed to get to know her quickly and was prancing on its back legs for her to pick him up again when they were leaving. Mrs. Glosner asked them to come back and see her and Jocko anytime. Melanie and Shane said they would.

The cat with the pushed-in face went to a man named Mr. Barton. Mr. Barton needed crutches to get around and had wanted a cat because they were easier to care for. Melanie saw tears in his eyes when they were leaving, and she and Shane promised they would visit him, too.

On the way to drop off Shane at his house before going on home, Jeffy had watched the outdoor

Christmas decorations they drove by, and Melanie had snuggled Rainbow up close in her lap. Beside her, Shane was quieter than usual.

"What are you thinking about?" she asked.

He smiled at her. "Pets, I guess. I never thought about not having a family before and having only a pet to talk to. Igor's great, but he's sure not a substitute for my mom and dad, no matter how weird they are."

"I know what you mean," she said. "You know, we promised both Mrs. Glosner and Mr. Barton that we'd visit them. I want to keep that promise."

"Me, too. We'll do it." Shane took her hand and folded it between his two. She rested her head on his shoulder. She had known that this was going to be a good Christmas for several people, including her.

"Where's Rainbow?" asked Jeffy, bringing Melanie back to the present.

"I imagine she's still in the basement," said his father.

"Oh, boy! She's missing all the fun." Jeffy scampered through the boxes and papers and headed for the basement.

"The poor thing's taking a nap," called Melanie. "Why don't you just let her rest? She's had a lot of excitement the past couple of days."

Jeffy ignored her and tromped down the basement steps. Melanie had just decided she would go to her room and listen to the tape when she heard Jeffy shout.

"HEY, EVERYBODY! COME HERE! COME HERE!"

Melanie followed her parents through the kitchen and down the stairs.

"Oh, my," her mother exclaimed.

Melanie peeked between her parents to see what they were looking at. There, in the bed that she and Jeffy had made for her, lay Rainbow and eight wiggling, squeaking little puppies, hardly bigger than mice. One was black, one was white, one was brown, and one was red, for each color in Rainbow's coat, and the other four looked exactly like her.

"They're beautiful!" cried Melanie.

Rainbow looked up at her, and Melanie could swear she was smiling.

"Now, that's what I call *pets*!" cried Jeffy.

"You haven't thrown away that list of people who need pets, have you?" asked her father.

"Larry! How could you think of giving these adorable things away," said her mother, kneeling down next to the box and picking up a puppy in each hand.

The rest of the family stared at Mrs. Edwards in disbelief for an instant and then turned to each other and smiled.

CHAPTER

15

"LOOK OUT!" yelled Jana as she tightened her grasp on her cafeteria tray to keep it from being knocked out of her hands. The girl who had run into her turned and stuck her tongue out and kept going.

Jana was shaking with anger when she reached the table where the rest of The Fabulous Five were sitting. "Did you see what Geena McNatt did?" she fumed. "She almost made me lose my lunch. I mean literally."

"Don't feel bad," said Katie, nodding. "She's making someone else's day right now."

Jana looked in the direction Katie indicated. Geena McNatt was in an argument with Tammy

119

Lucero at the other end of the room, and Tammy was wiping something off her skirt. It was obviously another bumping incident.

"The way she runs over people, she needs her own private traffic cop," said Christie.

"Remember what Jon said when Shane was talking her brother Max into donating to our animal fund," Beth reminded them. "He said all three of Geena's brothers were just like her. I guess it runs in the family."

It seemed to Jana that wherever Geena went, trouble followed. She was in Jana's Family Living class and was always disrupting things and picking on some of the smaller kids. The bumping incident was the first run-in that Jana had had with her. "Pardon my pun," she said, giggling, "but I really don't care to run into her again."

Jana does have another run-in with Geena McNatt. In fact she has to deal with the whole McNatt family. Find out how Jana handles the McNatt tribe in *The Fabulous Five #14: Seventh-Grade Menace.*

ABOUT THE AUTHOR

Betsy Haynes, the daughter of a former newswoman, began scribbling poetry and short stories as soon as she learned to write. A serious writing career, however, had to wait until after her marriage and the arrival of her two children. But that early practice must have paid off, for within three months Mrs. Haynes had sold her first story. In addition to a number of magazine short stories and the Taffy Sinclair series, Mrs. Haynes is also the author of *The Great Mom Swap* and its sequel, *The Great Boyfriend Trap.* She lives in Colleyville, Texas, with her husband, who is also an author.